D1524029

SPECIAL MESSAGE TO READERS

This book is published under the auspices of

THE ULVERSCROFT FOUNDATION
(Registered charity No. 264873 UK)

Established in 1972 to provide funds for
research, diagnosis and treatment of eye diseases.
Examples of contributions made are: —

A Children's Assessment Unit at
Moorfield's Hospital, London.

•

Twin operating theatres at the
Western Ophthalmic Hospital, London.

•

A Chair of Ophthalmology at the
Royal Australian College of Ophthalmologists.

•

The Ulverscroft Children's Eye Unit at the
Great Ormond Street Hospital For Sick Children,
London.

You can help further the work of the Foundation
by making a donation or leaving a legacy. Every
contribution, no matter how small, is received
with gratitude. Please write for details to:

**THE ULVERSCROFT FOUNDATION,
The Green, Bradgate Road, Anstey,
Leicester LE7 7FU, England.
Telephone: (0116) 236 4325**

In Australia write to:

**THE ULVERSCROFT FOUNDATION,
c/o The Royal Australian College of
Ophthalmologists,
27, Commonwealth Street, Sydney,
N.S.W. 2010.**

RIVERBOAT

When Rufus Blake died he was found to be carrying a gold bar from a Confederate gold shipment that had disappeared twenty years before. This inspires Wes Hardiman and Ben Travis to swap horse and trail for a riverboat, the *River Queen*, on the Mississippi, in an effort to find the missing gold. Cord Duval is set on destroying the *River Queen* and he has the power and the gunmen to do it. Guns blaze as Hardiman and Travis attempt to unravel the mystery and stay alive.

Books by Alan C. Porter
in the Linford Western library:

CORDOBA'S TREASURE

ALAN C. PORTER

RIVERBOAT

Complete and Unabridged

LINFORD
Leicester

First published in Great Britain in 1997 by
Robert Hale Limited
London

First Linford Edition
published 1999
by arrangement with
Robert Hale Limited
London

British Library CIP Data

Porter, Alan C.
    Riverboat.—Large print ed.—
    Linford western library
    1. Western stories
    2. Large type books
    I. Title
    823.9'14 [F]

    ISBN 0–7089–5475–8

Published by
F. A. Thorpe (Publishing) Ltd.
Anstey, Leicestershire
Set by Words & Graphics Ltd.
Anstey, Leicestershire
Printed and bound in Great Britain by
T. J. International Ltd., Padstow, Cornwall

This book is printed on acid-free paper

1

'Give yourself up, Blake, y'aint got nowhere to go,' Sheriff Frank Mardel of Harper's Ferry yelled. He was a slim man in his late forties clad in a dark, three-piece suit and shiny black boots.

'Come an' get me, Sheriff,' Blake invited. In the yard behind the livery stable, Blake crouched behind an old flatbed wagon. One front wheel had been removed and the wagon was propped up on an empty barrel.

A bullet slammed into the barrel and out the other side splintering wood and raising dust as it gouged into the ground.

It had been a mistake coming into town, but he needed supplies. How was he to know that some bright spark would recognize his likeness from an old dodger? But then life was full of little surprises, some, like this one, real nasty.

He peered around. Hemmed in by an assortment of ramshackle wooden buildings, he had nowhere to go.

'This is your last chance, Blake. Give yourself up,' Sheriff Mardel shouted.

'Go to hell!' Blake shouted back, fisting his Colt in a tighter grip, dark, mean eyes in a stubble-lined face darting about seeking movement.

Clad in dirty range clothes and scuffed boots, the grey duster he wore hung about his wiry, crouching figure like a dirty shroud.

There was movement on the edge of his vision to the left. Boots pounded on the hard-packed earth. A rifle cracked, the bullet slapping into the side of the flatbed just inches from his face, but the one doing the shooting, on the move as he fired, lacked accuracy. Blake was more methodical.

The pistol cracked twice and both bullets burrowed deep into the young and over-eager deputy's body, one bullet ripping through his heart before punching a bloody exit hole that shattered the deputy's shoulder-blade.

Blake felt a moment of satisfaction, but it was short-lived as men appeared in numbers from between the buildings, rifles and pistols spitting lead.

A dozen bullets smashed into Blake's body. He jerked upright for an instant as the bullets tore into his body from a dozen different directions at once, spinning and jerking him in an ungainly dance of death.

Blood, flesh and bone fragments jetted and sprayed in the warm, afternoon air and Rufus Blake, outlaw, murderer and robber was dead before he hit the ground, dying in the same violent manner as he had lived.

Sheriff Frank Mardel had seen it happen many times before and shook his head as he stared down at the bloody corpse. When would these men learn? The day of the outlaw was over; the West was changing fast and there was no place for them in it any more.

It was later, as Mardel went through the contents of Blake's saddle-bags, that he came upon something that made him wish that the outlaw had not died, something that sent him rushing to the telegraph office to send an urgent message to the state capital.

★ ★ ★

The girl was pretty and the mannish attire of jeans, boots and a baggy, yellow check shirt did little to hide her obvious feminine shape. Raven hair tumbled about her face from beneath the brim of a tan stetson.

Darkness had long since fallen over Mead's Crossing; she had not meant to be so late, Pa would be worried.

Her heels beat out a rapid tattoo on the planking of the jetty while, beneath, the Mississippi River sucked and gurgled about the stout pilings. Behind her, Duval's *Floating Palace*, an old, converted riverboat, filled the night with an oasis of light. She could

4

still hear the faint tinkling of a piano and raucous shouts mingled with girlish screams of delight, but the way ahead was entirely different.

A few lights streamed from the windows of the waterfront buildings, but these were few and far between. Most of the buildings she now passed were dark, unlit warehouses where an occasional lamp burnt high up on the wooden frontages to supply a welcome pool of light in the darkness.

It was all Mary Lou's fault. Her best friend had been away in Chicago for three months and had so much to tell that time had just flown by.

Jolene Pepper's heart fluttered as a shadowy figure rose up from a pile of crates then sank down out of sight. The shadowy world of the waterfront was a magnet of hoboes, drifters and drunks looking for a place to spend the night.

The lights of the *River Queen* appeared in the distance and her heart settled. In a few minutes she would be home and getting a cussing from Pa for worrying the life out of him, but that was preferable to the unseen dangers that lurked in the darkness.

During the day the waterfront was a bustling, lively place. Everyone knew everyone else and the waterfront maintained a rough, welcoming humour, but at night its mood changed. It became sullen and sly and dangerous.

Jolene fixed her eyes on the distant lights and continued resolutely on her way, quickening her pace a little.

'Well if'n it ain't Jolene Pepper.' The rough, amused voice came from a dark shape that suddenly stepped out in front of Jolene from a narrow alley between two buildings.

Jolene gave a startled shriek as she came to a stop, heart thumping in her breast, aware of two other figures slinking about on the edge of her vision, cutting off any chance of retreat.

'Jubal Tate, you gave me the fright of my life.' She tried to keep the fear from her voice, but it lingered in the

6

shrillness of her voice.

Jubal Tate finished the contents of a bottle and tossed it away and she heard it splash into the water. He was a big man, who topped the six foot mark by two inches, with broad shoulders and an even broader waistline. He always wore a black frock coat over a crumpled, blue suit and low-crowned hat on his brutish head from which tangles of greasy black hair fell almost to his dirty collar. His attire was his way of saying that he had come up in the world since his humble beginnings as a saloon swamper and waterfront labourer. He reminded Jolene of a cross between a preacher and an undertaker with the worst qualities of both.

He wiped the back of his hand across his mouth making the unshaven bristles rasp.

'What are you doing out this late, girl, looking for some fun?' he leered, whiskey-laden breath causing her to back up. He grabbed her arm in a vice-like grip.

'You let me be, Jubal Tate, or my pa'll . . .'

'You're pa'll what, girl? That old river rat ain't gonna do nothing.' He pushed her backwards violently so that she crashed heavily against the wooden frontage of a nearby warehouse, the action bringing her into the pool of light from a lamp above. He followed her. 'Reckon to have me some fun, girl,' he said thickly, reaching out a big hand and squeezing a breast painfully.

She slapped the hand away and inched along the wall, fear welling up inside her.

Jubal Tate laughed, but his laughter was cut short as a voice called, 'That'll be enough, Tate.' The words were accompanied by a hammer being pulled back.

Jolene's fear dissolved into relief. Solomon Jones, the Negro engineer of the *River Queen*, appeared on the edge of the light, a shotgun held in his hands. He was as big as Tate but without the stomach.

8

'Well, well. Ol' John Brown sure did the world a disfavour when he gave you Niggers freedom.'

Solomon's expression did not change.

'Bin looking out for you, Miss Jolene. You come along with me. Reckon this piece o' trash ain't gonna cause no trouble on accounts as that big belly is kinda hard to miss even wi' muh eyes closed.'

Jolene's smile of relief became a mask of terror as a shadow rose up behind Solomon.

'Solomon, look out!' she cried, but it was too late. something came down hard on the Negro's head and with a groan he crumpled to the ground from a blow delivered by one of Jubal Tate's two men.

'Ain't that a pure shame,' he grunted. 'Man's gotta have eyes in the back of his head on dark nights like this. Now, where were we?'

'You keep away from me you pig!' Jolene spat.

Her words brought a cruel gleam

into Tate's eyes. He lashed out with a hand catching her sharply on the side of the mouth, splitting the flesh so that blood welled darkly.

The blow rattled her head back against the wooden boards, stunning her slightly. Tate moved in knocking the hat from her head and grabbing a handful of hair at the back forcing her face up while his fat belly pinned her against the wall.

'Get rid o' that Nigger trash. Send him for a swim with some chains around his ankles. Got me some pressing business to attend to,' he called over his shoulder, and heard Solomon's unconscious body being dragged towards the darkened water's edge.

Jolene struggled uselessly against the weight that pinned her to the wall at the same time Tate was forcing her head back and using his free hand to knead and squeeze her breast.

Unable to scream or break free she was forced unwillingly to accept the vile attentions Jubal Tate was forcing on her. The one thought in her mind was that once Tate had finished with her she was going to kill him.

Foul breath washed hotly over her upturned face. She tried to turn away but he just increased his grip until it felt as though her hair was coming out at the roots.

Chains clinked vaguely in the background. There were thumps and bangs and tears sprang into her eyes as she heard Solomon splash into the river. As Tate lowered his face towards her she closed her eyes.

Jubal Tate's carnal desires were not to be realized. A hand that was even bigger than his own came from behind, clamped itself around his fat throat under the chin and jerked him savagely back. He released his grip on Jolene to paw at the hand about his throat that was cutting off his air and as she slid unceremoniously to the ground coming down heavily on her bottom, Tate was spun to face his opponent.

Jubal Tate always prided himself on his height and the way people always had to look up to him, even important people, now it was his turn to look up to someone who was a good head taller than him. He caught a momentary glance of someone clad in tan buckskin with silver hair spilling from beneath a hat set atop a grim, unsmiling face, then a fist like a small boulder came out of the night and exploded under his chin. The power of the blow lifted him off his feet and slammed him down heavily on the planking.

As Jolene viewed the buckskin giant with some awe, she was aware of a second figure approaching her. For a moment she felt a surge of panic thinking it was one of Tate's men, but he was a stranger clad in blue Levi's and a chestnut-brown hide jacket over a yellow shirt.

'Are you okay, ma'am?' There was genuine concern in his softly spoken voice as he helped her gently to her feet.

'I'm fine, but Solomon . . . ?'

'He'll be okay, 'cepting for a headache when he wakes up.'

'But I heard him go into the river.'

'Coupla boys got kinda careless an' fell in.'

'Who are you?'

'Name's Wes Hardiman an' the big fella's my pardner, Ben Travis.'

By now Ben had hauled the groggy Jubal Tate to his feet.

'Sure do hate me a man who mistreats ladies. Reckon you need to cool off, boy, but first you got some apologizing to do.'

'Go to hell!' Tate snarled, recovered enough to throw a punch at Ben, but it did not connect. The big man blocked it easily and returned the blow with far more devastating consequences that left Tate spread out on the planking of the jetty with a few loose teeth. When he was hauled to his feet a second time all the aggression had gone out of him. Ben propelled him towards Jolene and then held him upright by the back of his collar.

'Reckon you got somethin' to say to the lady,' Ben prompted. This time Tate was more careful with his words.

'Sorry, Miss Jolene, reckon I had too much to drink.'

'Guess that'll do,' Ben said brightly, then promptly marched Tate to the edge of the jetty and threw him into the cold waters of the Mississippi and then rejoined Wes and the girl.

Jolene, recovered from the ordeal, stared up with some awe as Ben swept his hat off to reveal his thick mane of silver hair that seemed to shimmer in the lamplight.

'How are you, ma'am?'

She had never been faced with a man the size of Ben before and it momentarily took her breath away. He was handsome, too, they both were. To cover her confusion she latched on to the word ma'am.

'Ma'am. I ain't no schoolteacher,' she cried indignantly. 'The name's Jolene, Jolene Pepper, Jo to my friends.'

'An' a right pretty name too,' Ben opined, with a smile that made her tingle all over. Any further pleasantries were cut short by a groan from Solomon. Ben moved across and helped him to his feet.

'Can you stand, fella?'

'Reckon I kin make it, suh.' Solomon probed the back of his curly head with a hand, wincing as he touched a lump.

'Oh, Solomon, your poor head.' Jolene darted across.

'It'll be fine, Miss Jolene, this ol' head's too thick to hurt for long.' He turned his eyes on Ben and Wes. 'I'm obliged for what you did for Miss Jolene. That Jubal Tate's a mean one. If'n you gen'lemen are staying in Mead's Crossing, you watch your backs now.'

'We always do, Solomon,' Wes replied. 'Now, which way you folks headed?'

Solomon pointed to the distant lights.

'To the *River Queen*, she's a steamboat that Miss Jolene's pa owns.'

'Best we get you there safe an' sound,' Wes said, handing Solomon back his shotgun.

'I'm obliged, suhs,' Solomon said. 'C'mon, Miss Jolene, your pa's fit to bursting.'

As the four moved off, three wet, bedraggled figures hauled themselves up a muddy bank. There was murder in Jubal Tate's eyes. He meant to get even and then some for the humiliation he had suffered at their hands and after that he would take his pleasure of that bitch Jolene Pepper.

'Git your hands up!' a rasping voice commanded as the four approached the gangway that led on to the deck of the riverboat, an old stern wheeler.

'Dammit, Pa, it's me, Jolene and Solomon,' Jolene called out.

'I hear you, girl, but I see four bodies.'

'I had a run-in with Jubal Tate and if'n it wasn't for Wes and Ben I don't know what would have happened.'

'S'right, Cap'n,' Solomon said. 'They done hit this poor ol' Nigger on the head somethin' shameful. They wus ready t' throw me in the river, but these two kind gents saved me an' Miss Jolene.'

'Name's Wes Hardiman, Cap'n Pepper,' Wes called out. 'My pard here is Ben Travis.'

2

'Move into the light so I kin see you,' the suspicious voice commanded. 'An' mind, I gotta gun.'

'Pa!' Jolene cried, as Wes and Ben moved to the end of the gangway that angled upward from the jetty on to the darkly shrouded deck of the steamboat. Here, at the head of the gangway a single lamp hanging from the underside of the upper deck cast a circle of yellow light.

'Feisty old critter, ain't he?' Ben whispered to Wes.

'An' I got good hearing too! Feisty am I?'

A dark shape materialized on the deck of the steamboat and a figure stepped on to the boards of the gangway causing the wooden slats to creak in unison with the soft gurgle of the water around the jetty pilings.

Captain Sam Pepper of the *River Queen* turned out to be a short, scowling figure, streamers of lank white hair tumbling untidily from beneath a peaked cap. He wore a thick jacket and toted a long-barrelled shotgun that he kept aimed at the two as he approached.

He stopped a few yards short of Ben and eyed the big man suspiciously.

'Kinda gives a fella a crick in the neck to look up at you, son,' he grumbled.

'Pa! Will you put that gun down. These boys saved me from Jubal Tate an' his men!' Jolene exploded from a position sandwiched between Ben and Wes.

'I heard you afore, girl, I ain't deaf,' Sam responded acidly, eyes flicking to Wes.

'Well, ain't you even gonna thank them?' Jolene demanded, stepping forward, hands on hips.

'What I oughta be doing is giving you a good whupping fer not getting back sooner. It ain't safe fer a girl to be walking these docksides at night.'

'Sorry, Pa,' Jolene said contritely. 'Guess I forgot the time talking with Mary Lou. It won't happen agin.'

Sam Pepper snorted and his expression softened a little as he looked as his daughter. He lowered the shotgun.

'Reckon I owe you fellas for helping Jolene.'

'Glad we could oblige, Mister Pepper,' Ben boomed out.

'*Cap'n*, young fella, Cap'n Pepper,' he snapped back. 'Step aboard. Got me some fine sipping whiskey if'n you've a mind to join me.'

A grin split Ben's face.

'Sure sounds fine to me, Cap'n. How 'bout you, Wes?'

'Lead on,' Wes replied.

Sam Pepper, with Jolene bringing up the rear, led Wes and Ben forward and up a narrow flight of steps on to the night-shrouded upper deck, Solomon having disappeared soon after boarding. From here, separated by a pool of darkness, could be seen the *Floating Palace*, as bright and gaudy as a Chinese New Year lantern. Ahead of them, light spilled from the first cabin set in a row that ran the length of the deck. Above them loomed the dark shapes of a single smokestack and the pilothouse as they approached the lighted cabin.

The main feature of the cabin was a large table with bench seats either side. Sam indicated that they should sit while he busied himself at a small, oak cabinet, returning with three glasses and a bottle and earning himself a pout from Jolene.

'Don't I get one too, Pa?'

'Dammit, girl, I brunged you up proper not to drink likker. It ain't ladylike,' he growled, taking off his cap and releasing a mane of tangled grey hair.

'Who said I was a lady?' she countered indignantly. 'Sides, I had me a shock an' need me something to settle my nerves.'

'Deserves you a whupping,' Sam growled, tossing the cap on to the table before sitting down facing Wes and Ben.

Unperturbed by her father's refusal, Jolene collected a glass and slapped it down defiantly with the other three.

Sighing, Sam proceeded to pour a generous measure into all the glasses except Jolene's, her measure being half the others. She looked as though she was about to say something, thought better of it and sat down next to her father.

'What brings you boys to town? You look to be more at home on a horse than a riverboat.'

'True, Cap'n,' Wes agreed, taking a glass. 'Ben an' me, we done just 'bout everything there is to do on land, thought we'd try our hand on the river.'

'Punched cows, built fences, sat in a saddle through rain an' snow; fried in the desert and froze in the mountains. Comes a time when a man looks for something new,' Ben took up the explanation.

'An' you reckon life would be easier on the river, eh?'

'No, sir, different,' Wes said, taking a sip of the whiskey and nodding his approval. 'Mighty fine whiskey, Cap'n.'

'Sure beats the cowtown gut-rot,' Ben said cheerfully, then realizing Jolene's presence gave her an apologetic look. 'Pardon me, ma'am. I'm forgettin' mysel' in the presence of a lady.'

Jolene smiled prettily. Ben had removed his hat and the lamplight sparkled in his silver hair.

'No apology needed, Ben. You should hear Pa when he gets going.' A wicked smile filled her face.

Her revelation brought a snort from Sam and suppressed smiles from Wes and Ben. Sam gave her a sharp, withering glare.

'Hush, girl!'

'Yes, Pa.' Jolene dipped her head and took a sip of her whiskey. The fiery liquid hit the back of her throat and she gasped and spluttered, her face turning a bright red.

Sam eyed her until she had recovered. 'Satisfied now?'

She nodded and brushed tears from her eyes looking a little shamefaced at the smiling Wes and Ben.

'I guess so, Pa,' she said huskily.

'So, you boys wanna ride the river, eh?' Sam returned to their former conversation.

'Beats getting saddle sores,' Ben said.

'I reckon I owe you for what you did for Jolene an' I'm in need of some extra crew just now.' He eyed them thoughtfully. 'Pay ain't much, but you get fed.'

'Suits us,' Wes replied.

'You gotta tell them, Pa,' Jolene spoke up, face serious.

Sam took a gulp from his glass and Wes and Ben exchanged puzzled glances and waited.

'Please, Pa,' Jolene begged.

'Dammit, girl, let a man think,' Sam growled.

Jolene's eyes flashed.

'Truth is, Pa and Cord Duval who owns the *Floating Palace*, have a feud going on. Pa's the last of the independent riverboat owners and Duval wants his franchise, one way or another.'

'Let me tell it,' Sam barked, reaching for the bottle and refilling the glasses. 'Was a time when there was a dozen or more o' us plying this stretch o' the river, then the railroads came and trade dwindled, but we managed to keep going until Duval stepped in. He wanted what was left of the river trade for himself and with men like Jubal Tate on his payroll it wasn't long afore the others were selling up.'

'Sounds a familiar story,' Ben cut in. 'Where we come from it's the big rancher buying or frightening out the smaller man.'

'Pa refused to sell up or be frightened off,' Jolene said proudly.

'Nigh on forty years I've been on this river an' the likes o' Duval an' his kind ain't gonna get their hands on the *River Queen*,' Sam said broodingly.

'Go on, Cap'n, you ain't said anything to change our minds yet,' Wes prompted quietly, and Ben nodded in agreement.

'Jubal Tate is only part of the problem,' Jolene said. 'He an' his boys control the docks. Max Haggar controls the river an' if anything he's worse than Tate.'

'That's a fact,' Sam spoke up. 'He cap'ns the *Creole Dancer* an' his ways ain't friendly. He's sunk more'n one boat by ramming it. Ain't no law riding the river to keep the peace, so Haggar makes his own law.'

'An' I was thinking how peaceful the river is,' Ben said.

Sam gave a short, hooting laugh.

'You gotta lot to learn 'bout the river, boy. She's mean an' moody. Make one mistake an she'll rip the bottom out of your boat an' rip the heart out of you.'

'An' on top of all that, there's the

26

river pirates,' Jolene cut in for good measure. 'They can board a boat in the middle of the night an' you wouldn't know until they slit your throat.'

Wes and Ben eyed each other.

'It's true, boys. Jus' like your stage robbers, only the river is their trail.' Sam eyed the two impishly from beneath shaggy brows. 'Still have a hankering for the river life?'

'Sounds more inviting than ever,' Wes said with a grin.

'When do we start?' Ben asked.

'If'n you're still interested, then be here at first light for that's when we'll be sailing.'

'We'll be here, Sam,' Ben promised.

★ ★ ★

In the early light of dawn the following morning the quayside was alive with activity. A thick, damp mist hung over the water enveloping the far bank in its grey, chilly folds.

With coat collars turned up, Wes and

Ben arrived and had their first daylight view of the *River Queen*.

She was an old, stern wheeler that had seen better days. The blue paint of her hull was cracked and flaking in patches and, unlike her modern counterparts with a rising deck structure of three or four levels and double smokestacks towering high above an ornate pilothouse, the *River Queen* had only two levels.

The upper level or promenade deck where the two had been the previous night was supported on a forest of twelve-foot, red-painted wooden uprights springing from the shallow-draughted hull of the boiler and cargo deck below.

Red was also the colour of the rails encircling the promenade deck and the catwalk around the pilothouse. Except for the row of white-painted cabins sprouting from the tan planking of the promenade deck and black smokestack, everything else was dark blue.

But the most awesome part of the

River Queen was the huge stern paddle with its alternate red and blue blades that rose a man's height above the level of the upper deck.

The *River Queen*, with a beam of twenty-five feet and length of a hundred feet, was small and plain in comparison with her bigger, more ornate sisters.

Ben exchanged a wry smile with Wes.

'We sure know how to pick 'em, pardner,' he commented.

Toting a carpetbag each they pushed through the swathe of sweating roust-abouts manhandling the waiting cargo for loading. Most of this seemed to be going in the direction of a big, double side wheeler called the *Creole Dancer* painted a gaudy red and white and twice the size of the *River Queen*.

They reached a knot of people and heard an angry voice cry, 'That cargo's mine, Tate.' The voice was that of Sam Pepper.

Glancing at each other the two pushed their way through the people in time to see the diminutive captain, his toes barely touching the planking of the quay, in the grip of the burly Jubal Tate who was lifting the irate river man by his coatfront. A few yards away, Tate's two cronies restrained Jolene by her arms.

Ben's expression darkened at the sight of her being held.

'Not any more, ol' man,' Jubal Tate snarled. 'You're trespassing an' this cargo's confiscated.'

'Who says?' Sam demanded, clawing ineffectually at the iron grip that held him.

'The law says, Pepper.' An elegantly clad man in a grey frock coat and a white, ruffle-fronted shirt pushed through the crowd from the left. He was flanked on either side by a pair of tall, darkly-clad individuals that Ben gaped at and shook his head in disbelief to make sure he was not seeing double, for the two were identical even down to the cold scowls that dominated their lean faces. Both wore thin, black leather gloves on their hands and wore a single, pearl-handled, Walker Colt tied low on their right hips. It was these two who did the pushing to allow the former through.

'The law of Cord Duval, I take it?' Sam spluttered.

'You could say that.' Duval smiled thinly. 'Let him go, Tate, and you two release the girl.'

Reluctantly, Tate released his grip and Sam darted forward to face Cord Duval while Jolene, on being released, turned on one of her restrainers and kicked him hard on the shins before moving to her father's side.

'You can't take my cargo, Duval.'

'Wrong. I can even take your boat, but that thing's not worth the taking.' Duval pulled a folded paper from his inside pocket. 'I now own this entire dock, bought and paid for, and you, Pepper, are trespassing, unless you can pay the mooring fee of one thousand dollars and with that you get your cargo back.'

There were gasps all round. Sam Pepper was rocked back on his heels by the news.

'You can't do that, Duval,' he choked, as Jolene came to his side.

'On my dock I can do what I like, old man,' Duval corrected. 'Can you pay the mooring fee?'

'You know we can't, Duval,' Jolene spoke up angrily, eyes flashing.

Cord Duval smiled.

'You are beautiful when you are angry, Miss Jolene, but business is business.' His handsome face hardened as he turned his gaze on Sam. 'A thousand dollars, Pepper, or you leave now, empty-handed.'

'I ain't got no thousand dollars an' I ain't leaving,' Sam said stubbornly. 'So what you gonna do 'bout it?'

'Then you'll lose everything, old man. My ownership of this waterfront is legal an' I've got the law on my side. I won't do anything. It'll be Sheriff Taplow who'll be doing the doing, so to speak. You'll end up in jail along with your daughter. After that I'll have that leaking bucket of yours towed into mid river and set fire to.'

'Dammit to hell!' Ben grunted, eyes flashing as the hands at his sides balled into huge fists.

Wes caught his arm.

'Steady, big fella. The two with Duval are the Lacroix brothers, a pair of hard gunsels with a reputation for being fast an' accurate.'

'We jus' can't stand by and see the cap'n hustled off his own boat,' Ben objected heatedly.

Wes smiled and pulled a thick wallet from his jacket.

'The time to play rough comes later. I reckon it's time to call Duval's bluff.' He pulled some bills from a thick wad in his wallet. 'Stay put an' look after my grip.' With that he returned the wallet to his inside pocket and stepped through the edge of the crowd.

The Lacroix brothers were aware of his approach before he had taken one step. Both turned, hands hovering over the butts of their Colts, eyes narrowed expectantly.

Wes smiled genially and lifted his hands chest high.

'Steady on, boys, I ain't got my hands filled with anything but money owed to Mr Duval.'

Duval turned at the sound of his name and stared suspiciously at Wes.

'Don't think I know you, mister.'

'The name's Wes Hardiman and I'm paying Cap'n Pepper's mooring fee. A thousand dollars you said.' He held the money out to Duval who hesitated to take it. 'I'm sure that you being a man of honour and not wishing to cause unnecessary hardship will be only too pleased to have this little misunderstanding settled to everyone's satisfaction and let the Cap'n have his cargo back?'

Fury flared briefly in Duval's eyes as a ragged cheer went up from the crowd. Forcing a smile he took the money.

'I'm a man of my word, Mr Hardiman.' He turned back to Sam

Pepper. 'You win this round, Pepper.' He turned back to Wes. 'I hope your investment is not wasted, Mr Hardiman. I look forward to meeting you again.'

'The pleasure will be all mine, Mr Duval,' Wes replied, as Duval turned on his heel and marched stiffly away, the Lacroix brothers at his side.

There was some applause from the crowd as it broke up and a smiling Ben joined Wes.

'That was some move, little fella. Never seen a fella looking more like he'd been kicked by a mule.'

'He talked himself into it when he wasn't expecting the fee to be paid,' Wes replied.

'That makes two of us, son,' Sam Pepper barked. 'How come you're willing to waste money like that?' Suspicion filled his eyes and words.

'Pa!' Jolene cut in. 'Wes has just saved you, the *River Queen* an' the cargo. I reckon that deserves a word of thanks.'

'Man don' hand out money unless he wants somethin',' Sam persisted. 'What's in it for you, son? I ain't got the money to pay you back.'

'Let's say I don't like seeing folks put on.'

'Let's say we put our cards on the table an' deal 'em as they come,' Sam growled. 'Man has to have a motive an' a thousand dollars must mean a pretty powerful motive.'

'Pa you're just being mean to the boys,' Jolene protested, but her words did not have her earlier conviction. Some of her father's caution had rubbed off.

'Whatever the motive, Cap'n, it means no harm to you. If'n it makes you feel any better, the money pays for Ben an' I to take a trip on the *River Queen*. No payback required.'

Sam Pepper eyed the two in puzzlement and finally shook his head.

'Ain't got the time to try an' figure what goes on in a cowboy's head, gotta cargo to get loaded. Welcome aboard the *River Queen*!'

With that he scampered away, yelling to a group of roustabouts to get the cargo loaded.

'I guess Pa said thanks,' Jolene said doubtfully.

'Sounded like it to me,' Ben laughed, and tossed Wes his grip.

'Best get you boys settled. We'll be sailing as soon as the cargo is aboard,' Jolene announced.

As the three boarded the *River Queen*, Wes paused to look back over the crowds that thronged the waterfront. There was no sign of Duval or his men. It should have made him feel relieved, instead he felt uneasy.

In truth, Wes had every right to feel uneasy for, even as he stood on the deck of the *River Queen*, Duval glowered down at him from the pilothouse of the *Creole Dancer*. Beside him stood a huge bull of a man, thickly bearded and topped with a mane of tousled, curly black hair.

There was a hard, vicious gleam in Duval's eyes.

'If'n I'm not much mistaken, Haggar, I reckon the *River Queen*'s about to make her last trip. That old fool Pepper's been stuck in my craw long enough.' A thoughtful look appeared in Duval's eyes.

Max Haggar grinned, teeth shining whitely in the black depths of his beard.

'This ol' river's mighty pernickerty, Mr Duval. She's like a woman. When she's good, she's good, but when she's bad she's all bad, an' I don't reckon the *River Queen* can take the bad.'

Cord Duval smiled. 'My feelings exactly.'

'What do you want me to do, Mr Duval?'

'Nothin', Max. We play this one carefully. Pepper's got friends here who could make life a tad uncomfortable if'n they thought we had anything to do with the unfortunate end of the *River Queen*. We stay here in full view of everyone. I've got a man on the payroll downriver who is now gonna earn his money.'

Duval left the *Creole Dancer* in a lighthearted mood that was positively genial as he walked between the sullen-faced Lacroix brothers back to the *Floating Palace*.

3

As the rising sun burnt away the early morning mist that hung over the river, the *River Queen*, rear paddle turning slowly, slipped its moorings and eased itself into mid river. Once in position, Sam Pepper turned her nose downriver, yanked on the steam whistle cord a few times and sent the riverboat surging forward.

Wes and Ben stood at the rail at the rear of the promenade deck that overlooked the huge stern paddle, looking down in fascination at the 'walking' beam engine that moved back and forth on its timber support trusses with a rhythmic thump and hiss as it turned the huge paddle. In turn, this was attached to a steam condenser and pipes that led back to the boilerhouse situated on the main deck below the pilothouse.

This was the reason that riverboats built upwards. The main deck was so cluttered with machinery and cargo that only the poorest traveller and crew occupied its limited space.

The two moved to the port rail and watched in silence as the huge, glittering *Floating Palace* slid by. It towered awesomely above the *River Queen*; twice as high and almost three times as long, its huge, redbladed side paddles added a flash of colour to the white-walled tiers. A few early morning gamblers, stretching their legs before returning to their endless poker games, paused to watch the *River Queen* pass. A group of saloon whores in gaudy dresses lined a rail and waved to the two.

Ben removed his hat and waved back cheerfully, the sun adding a shine to his silver hair.

'Ben Travis, I'm surprised at you!' Jolene's voice made both the men turn. There was an amused gleam in her eyes.

'Just being neighbourly, ma'am,' Ben said, nonplussed by her arrival.

Soon Mead's Crossing disappeared around a bend in the river and Wes and Ben climbed up to join Sam in the pilothouse. Behind them their passing was marked by a long, white wake churned up by the huge stern paddle as it turned.

As the sprawling civilization of Mead's Crossing vanished behind them, the thick, luxuriant vegetation on either side crawled to the very edges of the river and in some cases beyond. Invisible birds sang and chattered in the tree canopy, sometimes making themselves visible as a flash of colour as they dived for fish.

The scents that filled the air were new to the pair. For both men, brought up on the dry, arid plains and deserts to the west, the damp, vegetation-tinged air was a novelty.

Sam Pepper kept the *River Queen* in the centre of the river.

'Sure is a peaceful way of life,' Wes

observed later, after Ben had gone down to give Solomon a hand to keep the big boiler stoked. His remark brought a chuckle to Sam's lips.

'You don' wanna take this ol' river for granted, Wes. She might look peaceful, but underneath she's jus' biding her time, getting you all comfortable. You gotta watch for 'snags' and 'sawyers' or you'll have no bottom left in your boat.'

'How come the river is a *she*, Pa, an' not a *he*?' Jolene appeared in the pilothouse with tin mugs of hot, strong coffee for the two.

Sam scowled at his daughter.

' 'Cause she is, girl. Pretty on the surface, but scheming below, jus' like a woman, unpredictable!'

Wes turned away to hide a grin.

'Well it ain't fair,' Jolene argued. 'Men are jus' as bad an' in cases like Duval an' Tate, twice as bad.' With that pronouncement on men delivered she flounced out of the pilothouse.

Sam gave Wes a pained expression.

'See what I mean?' He shook his head and returned his gaze to the river ahead.

'What are these snags and sawyers, Sam?' Wes asked, referring back to their earlier conversation.

'Trees, son, trees,' Sam said grimly, causing Wes to frown his puzzlement.

Sam shook his head.

'They can tear a boat to pieces in the wink of an eye. Most o' the time you can't see 'em an' when you can, then it's too late. It's the trees you see, son. They get pulled in by the water, dragged under 'til they get caught on a sandbank or tangled wi' another tree. The branches point the opposite way to the run o' the water. The water hardens and sharpens 'em an' they wait below the surface like claws ready to rip the guts outa any boat that gets too close to 'em. We call 'em snags.' Sam paused to take a gulp of his coffee.

'How'd you know where these snags are, Cap'n?' Wes asked softly and Sam shrugged.

'You spend a lifetime on the river an' trust to instinct.' He cocked an eye at Wes. 'Still gotta itch to ride the river?'

'I'm scratching on it,' Wes replied. 'How 'bout the others you mentioned?'

'Sawyers?' Sam gave a cackle. 'Trees agin, son, allus trees, but sawyers, they don' wanna let go of the land so they hold on tight wi' their roots and bob up an' down an' can smash a hole in the side afore you know it. Crush a man to death if'n he falls in their path.' Sam shuddered. 'Had it happen on the old *River Queen* one time. Fella went overboard an' tried to make it to the bank. Lordy! Reckon you could hear the snapping o' his bones a mile away.'

'Dammit, Sam, you keep away from them sawyers,' Wes cried.

Sam laughed.

'I intend to, Wes.'

'Anything else I should know about?' Wes asked, casting Sam a sideways glance.

' 'Gators. Now they can bite a man in half if'n he's foolish enough to get in the way of their jaws, but that's more Baton Rouge way. Don't get too many of them this far upriver.'

'That's a relief.'

'Got poisonous water snakes. Swell a man up like a balloon.' Sam threw Wes a glance, clearly enjoying the look of discomfort clouding the young man's face. 'Then there's them river pirates that Jolene tol' you 'bout.'

Wes frowned. 'Cap'n, you paint a downright mean picture of river life. How come you still do it?'

Sam inclined his head.

'Take a look at the riverbanks an tell me where you'd find a purtier sight.'

Wes looked and on both sides of the river masses of white, pink-edged magnolias and scarlet azaleas mingled with the green of the trees for as far as the eye could see. In the sunlight, the magnificent blossoms seemed to glow and their scent filled the pilot-house

46

with a heady fragrance that he had not noticed before.

Wes nodded appreciatively.

'I see what you mean, Cap'n.'

★ ★ ★

It was towards evening that Sam brought the *River Queen* to a halt alongside a rickety looking jetty that fronted a row of straggling, clapboard buildings that Sam called Cutter's Landing. The small town served a community of cotton growers.

Willing hands appeared to help unload such cargo as was destined for the general store and saloon, then bales of cotton were loaded aboard to join the barrels of tar oil bound for Harper's Ferry.

By the time the last bale was loaded, darkness had already swallowed the far bank and was creeping across the river. Lights had sprung up in the town and piano music tinkled distantly from the town's single saloon.

'We'll stay here tonight and move on tomorrow,' Sam announced as they gathered on the lower deck. 'Annie's does real passable chow and Frenchie's saloon serves a real, decent brandy, all the way from France, if'n you boys are interested?'

'Reckon I could eat a horse,' Ben announced with a smile. 'An if'n Frenchies does a real decent beer that'll be even better.'

'Let's go eat,' Sam cried.

★ ★ ★

Gabe Deacon, hidden in the shadow of a single warehouse, watched as the group moved away from the *River Queen*, his dark, sunken eyes fixed on Jolene. As they left the jetty and headed into town, Gabe struck a match and held it to a long thin cheroot. The flaring light lit up his thin, smooth-shaven face with its prominent cheekbones that hinted of Indian blood somewhere in the past and indeed, his late grandmother had been a Chocktaw squaw.

Gabe sucked on the cheroot and blew smoke into the cool, night air. Whipcord thin, he dressed far above his humble position of jetty manager, maintaining the flashy elegance of a gambler in his dark suit and ruffle-fronted shirt that he topped off with a city derby. He considered himself a cut above the rest of the cotton-growing clods of Cutter's Landing; he was also Cord Duval's man, but he kept that knowledge to himself.

It was an arrangement that suited him well. He got paid by the townsfolk to run the jetty and also by Cord Duval.

He had, in the past, been called upon by Duval to arrange 'accidents' to befall other riverboat owners; now Duval had called upon him again. The telegraph had come during the morning. It bore the simple message: EXTEND RIVER QUEEN WARMEST WELCOME STOP. It had been addressed to him and signed simply, D.

Innocuous enough to the eyes of the telegraph operator, the message conveyed to him was far more deadly. For the moment he took his mind off the message and let it dwell on the raven-haired Jolene Pepper.

She was the subject for whom he had once harboured a secret longing in his dark soul. He had approached her openly on the matter, considering himself a very important man in Cutter's Landing; a catch for any woman and it had hurt his pride when she had rejected him. It was a hurt that still rankled now, but after tonight things would be different. He was about to avenge his damaged ego.

He smiled to himself in the darkness. Tonight she would pay for rejecting him. They all would. The sharp-tongued Sam Pepper and that stuck-up Negro Solomon Jones.

He tossed the butt of the cheroot away and headed into town. Already the jetty was almost deserted, by the time he had had a drink or two and returned he would have the jetty and the *River Queen* to himself.

★ ★ ★

'Yessir. Old Billy Duggan an' his steamboat sailed around the bend an' were never seen or heard of agin!' Sam nodded as he finished one of his long river stories and downed the contents of his glass.

They had all dined well at Annie's and now in Frenchie's saloon over well-filled glasses of brandy, Sam Pepper was at his verbose best. It seemed to Wes, as the story came to an end, that most of the saloon clientele had gathered around their table to hear the story.

'Never seen agin, Cap'n?' Ben questioned.

'Never, Ben, 'ceptin' on days when the fog lies heavy on the river, folks have heard the whistle of his old

51

steamboat deep in the fog. Heard the sound o' paddles slapping at the water, but never seen him.' Sam leaned forward conspiratorially and lowered his voice. 'Heard him mesel on more'n one occasion.'

Ben's eyes popped.

'Hell, if'n that don' beat all,' he growled.

* * *

As Sam recounted his story in the saloon, Gabe Deacon had returned to the deserted jetty and slipped aboard the *River Queen*. On the far side of the stack of cotton bales, hidden from view of anyone who might happen on the jetty, he emptied the contents of a can of kerosene over the bales, wrinkling his nose as the powerful fumes washed over him.

'What youse doing, mister?'

The voice coming suddenly from behind froze Deacon to the spot as the last few drips fell from the can.

Heart thumping in his chest, he half turned to see Solomon approaching. The big Negro had left the group after eating at Annie's and had returned to the *River Queen*.

Solomon sniffed the pungent fumes and his face creased. In the pale light of a half moon he saw the can still clutched in the other's hand.

'Tha's kerosene, mister. Hey, I knows you.'

Solomon's words ended abruptly as Deacon swung the empty can in a vicious arc. It caught Solomon across the side of the face, crumpling under the impact.

Solomon went down, cracking his head hard against a barrel of tar oil and lay still.

Breathing heavily, Gabe Deacon peered fearfully on to the jetty, but the jetty remained deserted. Calming himself he tossed the can into the river.

After a further cautious glance along the jetty to make sure it was still deserted he produced a short stub of candle that he lit and placed on the deck behind the bales. Carefully teasing a quantity of kerosene-soaked cotton from a bale he packed it around the base of the candle and, taking a final look at the unconscious Solomon, left the *River Queen*. It would take about five minutes for the flame to reach the soaked cotton wad then goodbye *River Queen* and goodbye the only witness.

In the shadow of the warehouse, he smiled to himself as he lit a cheroot and waited.

He had done his work well for it was not a long wait. A sudden orange glow flared in the darkness behind the bales. For a moment it seemed to dim, then with an audible whoosh the far side of the bales exploded in crackling, leaping flames that lit up the entire length of the *River Queen* and bathed the jetty in yellow light.

'That's what I call the warmest of welcomes,' he muttered.

★ ★ ★

'Pa! I heard tell Billy Duggan's alive an' well an' living in Natchez,' Jolene broke in.

Sam scowled at his daughter.

'Jus' goes to show you cain't believe everythin' you hear,' Sam riposted back.

'That sure is a fact,' Jolene retorted, fixing her father with a stare that brought a hoot of laughter from those gathered around the table listening to Sam.

It was laughter that was short-lived as Bart Fingle, who owned the general store overlooking the jetty, burst into the saloon, a mackinaw pulled over his nightshirt, naked feet thrust hurriedly into lace-up boots that he had not bothered to tie.

'Fire! Fire!' he bawled, causing all heads to turn. He saw Sam Pepper at the table and ran towards him. 'Fire, Cap'n. See'd it from my bedroom. The *River Queen*'s on fire!'

4

There was a momentary stunned silence that followed Fingle's breathless words, then pandemonium erupted in the saloon. Chairs crashed over as Wes and Ben leapt to their feet and raced to the batwings closely followed by Jolene and Sam and the rest of Frenchie's clientele.

The glow from the fire turned the sky over the jetty a lurid orange, providing a Hadean backglow to the row of buildings that backed on to the river.

Feet pounding the packed earth of the main street, the two cleared the obscuring buildings to catch their first sight of the burning *River Queen*.

Flames danced from the centre of the steamboat, licking the underneath of the promenade deck and curling upwards to blacken the rails above and sending red, moving shadows over the jetty. Above the flames, clouds of black, eye-stinging smoke drifted over the face of the moon. A few people had already appeared on the jetty and were standing gaping at the fiery spectacle, not knowing what to do. Only one man seemed to be doing something and both heard his voice as they ran across the rattling planking towards the *River Queen*. The man carried an axe.

'You men find poles. I'll cut the moorings and you push her into the river or she'll set fire to the jetty!'

'No!' Sam wailed from behind.

'We've got to find Solomon!' Jolene shouted to Wes and Ben.

'I'll find him,' Ben called. 'Stop that fella wi' the axe, Wes.'

'Watch yoursel', Ben,' Wes called, as he veered in the direction of Gabe Deacon.

Deacon had reached the wooden capstan that the thick mooring line had been wound around and had raised the axe over his shoulder when he felt it grabbed and torn from his hand from behind. The move almost unbalanced him.

He staggered back, waving his arms, managing to turn and still keep upright. There was a faintly amused glint in Wes's eyes as Deacon glared at him.

'You hold on a minute fella,' Wes said.

Deacon recognized Wes as being from the *River Queen*.

'Ain't gotta minute, mister. There's barrels of coal oil on that boat. If'n they explode the whole town'll go up. Gotta cut her loose an' get her away from here.'

At that moment Sam came puffing up.

'Ain't no fancy pants cutting my boat adrift,' he raged.

'You old fool. Folks are gonna die if'n the town burns an' it'll be on your head,' Deacon shouted.

'I'll go help, Ben,' Wes said to Sam. 'Keep your eye on this ranny.'

Sam smiled mirthlessly as he tugged an old derringer from inside his coat and pointed it at Deacon.

'Might not be much, Gabe Deacon, but from this range it'll sure put a hole in you. Now why don't you smoke one o' your cigars an' let us handle this.'

'Damn fool. I ain't gonna stand here an' git burnt to death, gun or no gun.' With that Deacon turned on his heels and darted away. A feeling of panic enveloped him. Events had started to go horribly wrong. The Negro on the boat had recognized him. He should have taken care of him properly, for now, if the man survived, the finger would be pointed firmly in his direction.

Sam stared after the retreating Deacon and shrugged, then became aware of the ring of men surrounding him and he stirred himself into action. Forgetting Deacon he hollered, 'You men follow me, we gotta boat to save!'

Ben had already found the unconscious Solomon and was carrying him from the boat when Wes arrived with Jolene in tow. Lowering Solomon gently to the ground he called to Jolene.

'Take care o' him, ma'am.' He turned to Wes. 'Fire's on the river side of the boat. Need to get them barrels moved an' any bales not alight. I'll take care of the others.'

'Go, big fella, I'll handle the barrels.' Wes turned to a group of men as Ben darted back aboard. 'Help me get them barrels moved.' He threw the axe aside and charged up the creaking gangway, disappearing into a cloud of smoke.

The men hesitated until Jolene shouted, 'Go help the man you yellow-livered skunks!'

They looked at each other then followed in Wes's wake. The smoke cloud had drifted away enabling them to see Wes as he staggered towards them, a barrel clasped to his chest.

'Form a line an' pass the barrels down,' he yelled hoarsely, tears streaming from smoke-reddened eyes.

On the other side of the *River Queen*, Ben shielded his face against the glare and heat of the flames with one big hand as he surveyed the situation, a boathook gripped in the other.

The outer wall of bales blazed from one end to the other in a crackling curtain of flame that reflected in a shimmering blanket of gold far out into the river. He had to get rid of those bales before they set the whole pile alight.

Using the boathook he yanked the nearest top bale from its perch sending it slamming to the deck in a fierce explosion of sparks. It landed on its burning face. He dropped the boathook and heedless of the flames licking upwards he got his fingers under the bindings holding the bale together and with a mighty heave lifted it clear of the deck and threw it over the side into the river.

The heat was intense, forcing him to retreat down the deck between each successful jettison of a burning bale. With flesh stinging and prickling from the heat he slapped at smouldering patches that appeared on his clothing.

The leaping flames reflected redly in

the slowly moving water as a half-dozen bales, some still burning, drifted out into the river, sinking lower and lower as the cotton absorbed the water.

On the other side of the bales, all the barrels had been moved to a place of safety on the jetty. Sam had brought more men and now the cotton bales, untouched by the flames, were being dragged clear.

Ben leant on the rail, sweat streaming from his smoke-blackened face, gasping air into his heaving lungs. He never realized how something as light as cotton could weigh so much when it compressed into bales.

The seventh burning bale had just gone over, taxing his great strength to the limit. He shook his head, dragged in a deep breath of clean air and moved forward. So far he had been lucky in that the bindings had held around the bales enabling him to get a grip, but that luck would not last forever.

On the eighth bale it ran out.

The left-hand binding snapped as he

swung the bale on to the rail, setting free the cotton heads that flared into brief, burning life, dropping around his feet and floating down to the water in a fiery cascade.

Ben released his grip on the remaining binding and let the disintegrating bale plunge into the water.

Exhaustion sent Ben to his knees, arms flung out over the rail for support. The flickering glare of the last six bales in two piles of three, fell over him. He could hear jubilant voices from behind as the last bales, untouched by the fire, were dragged clear of the inferno.

A pair of hands came under Ben's armpits as Wes appeared and hauled his friend to his feet.

'You all right, Ben?' Concern was mirrored in Wes's face as he turned his big partner around. Ben managed a grin, tears streaming from his smoke-reddened eyes.

'Cooked to a turn,' he croaked hoarsely.

'Look out!'

The urgent cry snapped Wes's head around. The bindings on the bottom line of burning bales had parted causing the bales to collapse beneath the weight of those above. Now the piles had begun to topple towards the two men.

Ben, his eyes still streaming was not immediately aware of the danger, but gave a yell of surprise as he felt himself propelled backwards by Wes over the rail and both men plunged into the water.

Two of the bales hit the rail and broke apart in an awesome cascade of white flame. Black smoke exploded a rain of flaming cotton heads that dropped into the water after the two. Others flew along the deck, burning brightly and fiercely before winking out.

Jolene, followed by the now recovered Solomon, came aboard in time to see the bales collapse on to the two men and she screamed.

Sam Pepper shouted, 'Douse them

flames an' you, come wi' me'. He pointed to half a dozen of the men nearest before dashing to the side of the boat, eyes searching the water below. 'Ben, Wes!' he bawled at the water.

'There they are!' a man called.

'Git boathooks!' Sam ordered, moving along the side to where two heads had surfaced.

A few minutes later, Wes and Ben were hauled on board the *River Queen*. Sam grabbed Ben's hand as the two were helped to their feet.

'Never seen the like o' it afore, Ben, you toted them bales as if they weighed nothin. You saved the *River Queen*, both of you.' He transferred his grip to Wes's hand, a smile stretching his whiskered lips. Jolene came forward and hugged both the men, giving them both a kiss, mindless of their dripping condition.

'You were wonderful,' she added to her father's praise.

'All in a day's work,' Wes responded, grinning broadly, retrieving his hat from where it had fallen, knocked from his head by Ben's flailing arm as they had plunged overboard.

'My hat!' Ben moaned, clapping a hand to his silver hair that was plastered about his head and face.

'I got it for you, mister,' a voice called out. 'See'd it floating away an' fished it out.' A man pushed through the ring of onlookers and handed Ben his hat.

'That's right neighbourly of you, friend,' Ben acknowledged with a broad grin, clapping the hat on his head and feeling all the better for it.

'Pa, you gotta hear what Solomon has to say,' Jolene spoke up.

'All in good time, girl. You men help git the rest of them flames out.' By now the four remaining bales were almost out as men scooped up buckets of river water and threw them over the flames. 'So, what in tarnation happened here, Solomon?' Sam rounded on the Negro as the ring of men broke up to help douse the final flames.

'Was that jetty man, Cap'n: Gabe Deacon. I caught him pouring lamp oil over the bales an' when I challenged him, why he up an' hit me wi' the can.' Solomon rubbed the side of his head.

'You mean it was deliberate?' Sam choked, appalled at the thought.

'Yessir, Cap'n.'

'Thought I could smell kerosene,' Ben said.

'But why? Deacon's been jetty master here for years. I don't get it. Where's that goddamn sheriff?'

'I'm here, Sam.'

A man, red-eyed with a smoke-blackened face, pushed himself forward. Sam hadn't recognized Sheriff Rafe Small in the confusion of people helping to save the *River Queen*.

Sam took the sheriff's arm and quickly related Solomon's story.

'Reckon we should have a talk with Deacon,' Small said grimly, running a hand across his moustachioed face, streaking the soot that darkened it.

'Anyone seen Gabe Deacon?' He raised his voice, but the question only brought forth a series of negative head shakes from those within earshot. 'He has a place over the warehouse,' Small cried. 'Come on, we'll pay him a visit an' see what he's gotta say for hisself.'

But they were too late. Gabe Deacon had seen how things were going and had not hung around to await the inevitable. Long before the fire on the *River Queen* had been put out, he had beat a hasty retreat.

It was evident from the untidy state of the two rooms over the warehouse that someone had done some rapid packing.

'Guess he's long gone,' Wes said woefully.

'We'll git him,' Sheriff Small declared. 'I'll git some messages off to the nearest towns. He'll turn up somewhere an' when he does he'll have a whole heap of questions to answer.' The sheriff shook his head dolefully. 'Ain't no end of wanted varmints on the loose at the moment. The bank was robbed at Georgetown two days ago by the Ike Mason gang, three men killed.'

As the group returned to the jetty, Gabe Deacon was some ten miles north of Cutter's Landing and heading on horseback towards Mead's Crossing.

★ ★ ★

The following morning was well advanced by the time the cargo had been restacked and Sam eased the *River Queen* away from the jetty at Cutter's Landing and headed downriver. The only evidence of the previous night's fire was a charring of the underneath of the promenade deck and blackening of the rails immediately above the fire area.

Apart from aching muscles and a few minor burns, Ben was up and about early to help Solomon get up a head of steam from the *River Queen*'s wood-burning boiler.

Sheriff Small came to see them off.

'Had a talk wi' the stable boy at the livery an' it seems that Deacon came by, saddled his horse and lit out. The boy said he was heading north an' that means Mead's Crossing. I've sent a telegram to the sheriff there to keep an eye out for him. Reckon he'll be in jail by tonight.'

'Jail's too good for that varmint; I'm obliged, Rafe,' Sam said.

'Drop by on your way back an' I'll let you know what happens.'

But fate had other plans for Gabe Deacon, for as the *River Queen* cast her moorings, Cord Duval had a visitor in his opulent suite aboard the *Floating Palace*.

Simpkins, a flabby, bespectacled man who ran the Mead's Crossing telegraph office, presented himself to Duval.

'Thought you might wanna see this afore I deliver it to the sheriff, Mr Duval.' He handed Duval a flimsy.

Cord Duval's handsome face darkened with anger as he read the message addressed to Sheriff Baker. It ran thus: ARREST GABE DEACON STOP WANTED IN CONNECTION WITH FIRE ABOARD THE RIVER QUEEN STOP. It was signed: RAFE SMALL, SHERIFF. CUTTER'S LANDING.

Duval passed the message back before reaching into his inner jacket pocket and drawing out a thick wallet. Simpkins eyed the wallet greedily and licked his lips in anticipation. Duval extracted a twenty-dollar bill and held it up, smiling at the man.

'You did well, Simpkins. Wait an hour before delivering the message to the sheriff.' Duval offered the money.

'You can count on me, Mr Duval,' Simpkins replied, taking the money and grinning happily.

'I hope I can,' Duval replied pointedly.

After the man had gone Duval called the Lacroix brothers into his private sanctum.

'Our friend Deacon has messed up. He's on his way here. Ride out and meet him and make sure he gets here safely.'

By noon, Cord Duval had the answer he didn't want. The *River Queen* was unharmed. Deacon had failed completely and Duval was not a happy man.

5

'Can't get over that Gabe Deacon.' Sam shook his head. 'Why in tarnation would he do such a thing?' Sam looked from Wes to Ben for an answer.

It was much later that day. The three stood at the forward rail on the upper deck below the pilothouse. Ahead, the seemingly endless river meandered on and on between thickly wooded banks. In the pilot-house Jolene was at the wheel.

Sam had laughed at the pair's expression when he joined them on the deck.

'She's bin at the wheel of the *River Queen* since she wus thirteen. Truth is she's as good as me, but that's 'tween you an' me.'

With the previous evening's events and Cutter's Landing far behind them, only the questions remained.

73

Wes turned from leaning on the rail, gazing at the sun dappled river ahead, and sat on it, arms folded across his chest.

'Seems to my way of thinking that the man was paid to do it,' he mused.

'Paid? Who in damnation would pay someone to burn the *River Queen*?'

'I can think of one man,' Ben answered, still leaning on the rail gazing ahead.

Sam snapped his head around in the other's direction.

'Who you got in mind, son . . . ?' His voice trailed away and his eyes widened. 'You ain't meaning Cord Duval?'

Ben looked across at Wes.

'Is that your way o' thinking, partner?'

'Spot on, big fella. 'Course proving it would be a mite difficult, but wi' Deacon on the run now he might just be inclined to spill the beans to save his own neck, if'n the law catches up wi' him first.'

74

'Could be blood he'll be spilling if'n he gets to Duval,' Ben said grimly. 'Cord Duval strikes me as the kinda fella who gets rid of his mistakes an' right now Deacon is the biggest mistake he's made.' Ben would not know until much later how prophetic his words were for, unbeknown to any of them, at this very moment Gabe Deacon floated face down in the water just outside Mead's Crossing.

'You reckon Deacon is Duval's man?' Sam questioned.

'Well if'n I was on the run, the last place I'd be heading for is Mead's Crossing unless I had reason to believe that someone there was gonna help me,' Wes cut in.

'It makes sense now.' Sam nodded his head. 'Two boats over the last three years have got burnt out at Cutter's Landing.'

'An' I bet they belonged to men who wouldn't sell out to Cord Duval?' Wes eyed Sam expectantly.

'You'd win your bet,' Sam agreed.

'Gabe Deacon . . . a Duval man. I'd never have believed it.'

'Point is, how many other men down this river work secretly for Duval?' Ben posed the question that neither could answer.

'Guess we're gonna have to watch our backs a tad more closely,' Wes finally broke the silence that had fallen.

'Ain't no worry 'bout that when we stop for the night at Jesse an' Corabel's,' Sam vouched. 'Ain't but Jesse an' Corabel there.' Sam gave a cackle.

'How's that, Sam?' Ben questioned.

'It's where we take on wood for the boilers, son. The *Queen* has a powerful hunger for logs, so we have to stock up at various points along the river. Some places we'll be cutting our own, but here ol' Jesse will have a stack waiting. At one time all the farmers along the river would make a few dollars extra cutting an' selling logs, but like I said afore, the steamboat trade ain't what it was twenty years back. Just ain't enough trade to go round these days.' There was a forlorn note in the old captain's voice.

'Deck seems pretty loaded wi' cargo to me, Cap'n,' Ben ventured. His remark brought a derisive laugh from Sam.

'Back in the old days, cotton bales'd be stacked so high all you'd see of a riverboat was the pilothouse. The *Queen*'s a small boat, a hundred foot from prow to paddle. Now you take Duval's *Creole Dancer*. She's three times the length an' twice the height. I've seen her piled high wi' cargo an' then have to leave the same amount behind for a second trip. But not now. She don't carry much more'n we do an' that's no good for a boat that size.'

'Could be why Duval is so all fired eager to get control of the river, if'n the trade is that bad,' Wes pointed out. 'Get rid of the competition an' what there is, is his.'

'Son, you make horrible sense,' Sam said glumly.

'How long has Duval been in Mead's Crossing, Sam?' Wes asked.

'Twenty-five, twenty-six years. He came with the Confederate Army an' stayed when the war was over.'

'Duval was in the Confederate Army?' Wes threw Ben a look.

'Sure was. Came as a major. Used to be a lot of troop movement up an' down the river then, an' supplies for the feds.'

'That's mighty interesting,' Wes breathed thoughtfully.

'Sure is,' Ben agreed. The tones of both men had Sam looking from one to the other in puzzlement.

'You boys mind letting an ol' river captain in on the secret?'

Wes unfolded himself from the rail and stared out over the river ahead. He seemed to be thinking and both men watched as finally he came to a decision. He turned to Sam.

'Ever hear of the *Southern Belle*, Cap'n?'

'Hear of it! I see'd it when it came

into Mead's Crossing twenty-five years ago.' A broad smile stirred his whiskers as he looked from one to the other. 'You boys is a-looking for the *Southern Belle*. I should'a guessed it. Folks have bin looking for that ol' boat since it disappeared carrying with it a million dollars of confederate gold bullion. Ha! You had me fooled there, boys. Never pegged you for a couple of treasure seekers.'

'So it was here the same time as Duval?' Wes prompted.

'Sure was, an' I kin tell you now, you's wasting your time. It's bin looked for by the best. Even looked for it mesel, one time. Ain't no one ever found it an' I reckon no one will.'

'What happened to the *Southern Belle* exactly?' Ben asked.

'Exactly, Ben? She steamed out of Mead's Crossing one June night bound for Harper's Ferry an' was never seen agin. There was a thick mist on the river that night an' they say she must'a hit a snag and sunk.' Sam shrugged.

'All they ever found o' her was the paddle an' that was at Butler's Point an' we passed that on the first day out.'

'Well you're wrong 'bout it not being found, Cap'n. Coupla months ago, the law in Harper's Ferry had a shootout with an outlaw called Blake,' Wes said.

'I heard 'bout it,' Sam said with a nod.

'What you never heard 'bout was the law finding a gold bar in the outlaw's saddle-bags. It was stamped with a confederate mark an' other markings identified it as belonging to the consignment carried by the *Southern Belle*.'

Sam's eyes widened. 'You don' say,' he breathed.

'It looks like Blake found the missing bullion, but where died with him. Ben an' I were sent to find it.'

'Sent?'

'The government has more than a passing interest in finding the gold.'

'You boys are government agents?' Sam whispered in awe.

'Let's say we sort out problems for them an' leave it at that, Cap'n. We're just a couple of boys tired of the land an' looking for a new life on the river. Be obliged you keep the rest to yourself, especially the finding of the gold bar.'

'Figured you were more than you said when you paid Duval the thousand dollars. Don' worry, your secret's safe wi' me. 'Sides I owe you boys, you saved the *River Queen* an' for that I'm beholden.'

Any further conversation was cut short by the steam whistle above giving vent to a long, throaty hoot followed by two shorter blasts that had birds screeching out of the trees on the nearer bank and making the three jump.

Jolene stuck her head out of an open light in the pilothouse.

'Jesse's place coming up, Pa!' she shouted down.

'Take her in slow an' easy, girl,' Sam hollered back.

There was no landing stage here, just an earth bank that had been cleared of vegetation. Jolene brought the *River Queen* in gently, expertly, the rear paddle slowing and finally stopping letting momentum carry her in. The side of the boat scraped along the bank to aid the slowing process.

Wes and Ben broke forward and aft to leap ashore with the mooring lines under Sam's guidance. Once ashore the lines were secured to a pair of tree stumps and Sam lowered the gangway and joined the two ashore.

He peered about worriedly.

'Ain't like Jesse not to be here,' he growled.

Around them the approach of night was more in evidence as the tree surround cut off the waning light and filled the clearing with a dusky gloom. To one side, a stack of freshly cut logs was piled high.

'Where's Jesse, Pa?' Jolene asked, as

she came down the gangway.

'Best find out I reckon,' Sam said and set off with the others in tow, along a worn, narrow path between the trees. They emerged a few minutes later in a wide clearing at the centre of which stood an old log cabin, one end partially cloaked in ivy. The cabin was in darkness.

'Jesse, Corabel, it's me, Sam Pepper,' Sam called out as he approached the cabin.

Hidden by the trees the sun had set. Overhead, the blue sky had turned violet and was rapidly darkening to give a brief dusk.

All around them darkness was spilling from the trees.

Sam mounted the wide porch with its pair of rockers and tried the door. It opened at a touch and swung slowly back to reveal the darkness within.

'Jesse!' Sam called into the darkness.

Behind Sam, Wes sniffed the dry, warm air that came from within. There was a peculiar, metallic taint that set the alarm bells ringing in his head.

'Hold it, Sam,' Wes caught Sam's arm and pulled him back. 'Get the lamp, Ben.' He nodded towards an unlit lamp that hung above the porch while Sam eyed him with questioning eyes.

The lamp sprang into life as Ben applied a match.

'Best you an' Jolene stay back,' Wes said quietly as he took the lamp, and something in the younger man's voice killed any protest the old man might have voiced.

Holding the lamp out in front Wes, followed by Ben, entered. The glow from the lamp filled the tiny room they found themselves in with a bright, cheery light that sent the night shadows scurrying back into the corners and up into the roof angles beyond the timber beams. It also fell across the room's occupants: a man and a woman in their late sixties.

She lay face down on the floor while he lolled in a chair before a wooden table on which the remains of supper still lay. Both were dead. Blood was splashed everywhere and lay in large, congealing pools about the body of the woman. It was the scent of blood that Wes had detected on the air.

The old man only remained upright because of the ropes that bound him to the chair. His throat had been cut, blood spraying the table top before it had soaked his shirt front and lap and pooled in the seat between his legs.

'Oh, dear God!' Sam's anguished cry followed by a shocked, stifled scream from Jolene came from the doorway as the two followed Wes and Ben.

Ben turned quickly from the hideous sight and moved towards the two, spreading his arms to prevent them entering further.

'Best you stay outside, Cap'n, Jolene. Wes an' I'll take care of things here.' He ushered them out, past a wide-eyed, staring Solomon.

'Who'd do such a thing, Ben?' he whispered hoarsely. 'They wus good folks. Never did no harm to anyone.'

'Don' know yet, Solomon. Take care of the cap'n an' Miss Jolene. Get them back to the *River Queen*. Wes an' I'll be along directly.' As he spoke Ben gently turned Solomon and eased him towards where Sam and Jolene stood in shocked silence.

A short while later the two dug a shallow double grave in the soft earth behind the cabin using spades found in a nearby outbuilding. They wrapped the two in blankets and buried them side by side before returning wearily to the *River Queen*.

'If'n that ain't the damnedest thing,' Ben said softly. 'Why would anyone wanna kill two old folks like that?' He shook his head in angry frustration.

'Did you see the old man's hands?' Wes replied, as the lights of the *River Queen* appeared through the trees ahead. 'The fingers on his right hand had been deliberately broken. Whoever killed them, tortured him first.'

'Ain't no way to die,' Ben said flatly.

'I'd like to get my hands on the rannies who did this.' He bunched his huge fists in the darkness.

The others were waiting on deck in a silent, tight-lipped group as the two came aboard. In the lamp-light tears sparkled on Solomon's and Jolene's cheeks and Sam's eyes were filled with water.

Wes told them what they had done and Sam nodded.

'That's real decent of you, boys. What kinda hell-spawned varmint does that to decent folks?'

'Guess we'll never know, Sam,' Wes said. 'They'll be long gone by now.'

'Not that long gone, boy, in fact not gone at all.'

The gruff voice came from behind and both Wes and Ben spun around as a dark figure came up the gangway followed by two others. The leading figure held a shotgun in his hands. 'Be obliged you boys shuck the gunbelts. I don' have to aim wi' this, jus' pull the trigger.' He stepped on to the deck and stopped. He was a tall, chunkily built man.

Thick strands of lank black hair spilled from beneath his hat reaching down to a full, ragged beard and curling over the collar of a long, dark coat. His small, mean eyes were almost lost in the shadow cast by his hat brim. Apart from the shotgun he carried a bulging saddle-bag over his left shoulder.

Two other men came from behind and arranged themselves on either side of him. Both were shorter than he and clad in drab, nondescript clothes.

The man nodded his approval as Wes and Ben let their gunbelts drop to the deck.

'That shows good sense, boys. They call me Ike Mason.'

'You robbed the bank in Georgetown,' Sam blurted out.

'See muh fame travels afore me,' Mason said with a smile. 'This 'ere's Joe Lascar.' He indicated with an inclination of his head the man to his left, a lean-faced individual with

88

cold, bleak eyes devoid of expression, lower jaw bristling with dark beard stubble. 'An' this 'un's Crazy Jack.' His head tipped the other way to a round-faced man with straggly blond hair tumbling from beneath his hat and intense, staring eyes. He uttered a curious, nervous giggling sound as their eyes fell on him.

'I take it you killed those folks in the cabin?' Ben spoke in brittle tones.

'Had to be done,' Mason agreed with casual indifference. 'When the ol' man told us Cap'n Pepper wus a-coming I saw me a chance to do a little river riding to beat the law.'

'Did you have to torture the old man to get the information?' Wes said tautly.

Mason gave a braying laugh.

'Hell, boy, he tol' us all we wanted to know afore Crazy Jack had his way. He do love to hurt folk an' gets real tetchy if'n he can't have his own way.'

'You oughtn't to have done that. No sir, that ain't right, ain't right at all.' It was Solomon who spoke, his eyes fixed hotly on Crazy Jack.

'Gotta tie up the loose ends, boy,' Mason said with a smirk. 'So, Cap'n Pepper, you an' this ol' scow have been commandeered. You're gonna take us down the river.'

'They wus good people an' you killed them!'

Something in Solomon's voice made Wes look at him. Tears were streaming down the big Negro's face. 'I's gonna kill you!' He leapt forward as he spoke taking everyone by surprise, wrapping his big hands around Crazy Jack's throat and slamming him against one of the red uprights that flanked the gangway.

For a few seconds confusion reigned. Crazy Jack pulled a thick-bladed Bowie knife, intending to use it on Solomon. Instead, Ben moved forward and shot out a foot, kicking the weapon from the man's hand. At the same time Wes made a move for his gun only to find himself looking down the barrel of a Smith & Wesson pulled by Joe Lascar.

Mason, in the meantime, as Ben kicked the knife from Crazy Jack's hand, drove the walnut stock of his shotgun hard into Ben's stomach. The blow sent the big man to his knees, the victory smile giving way to a grimace of agony.

Mason followed up using the shotgun as a cudgel and slamming it against the side of Solomon's head. The blow was enough to make Solomon release his grip and stagger back while Crazy Jack slid weakly to the deck, coughing and gasping, pawing at his throat.

Mason, face vicious, swung the shotgun butt again sending Solomon reeling to the opposite rail.

'Like I said, loose ends gotta be cleared up. I don' like loose ends an' I especially don' like Nigras,' Mason grated. He pulled a Colt Pioneer from a holster about his waist, raised it and fired.

Solomon gave a harsh cry, spun

unsteadily and disappeared over the rail into the water with a heavy splash.

Jolene screamed and Mason rounded on her.

'Loose ends, girl. Gotta be dealt wi' promptly,' he hissed.

6

'Well that was a howdedo an' no mistake,' Mason growled, returning the pistol to its holster and training the shotgun on Ben as the other rose to his feet.

'You murdering scum!' Sam Pepper raved.

'Careful ol' man or you'll be next,' Mason warned darkly. He turned his gaze on Crazy Jack. 'Git up, Crazy Jack, you make the place look untidy,' he said unsympathetically.

Crazy Jack rose to his feet gathering up his knife in the process, glaring murderously at Mason, who, if he noticed, paid no attention.

'Shoulda let me have him,' he rasped balefully, one hand still massaging his throat.

'That's why I shot him. Ain't got no time for you to mess 'bout.' Crazy

Jack fixed his boss with a hard look and Mason frowned. 'Don' go giving me no looks, boy, I ain't in the mood.' He looked back at the others. 'Ol' Crazy Jack, I swear he'd like to stick me wi' his knife at times.' He sighed and settled his sights on Sam. 'Time to get this ol' tub moving, Cap'n, or like as not we'll be having another burial at sea.' He chuckled at his own joke.

'Ain't possible,' Sam returned. 'Start moving this ol' tub as you call her, now, an' like as not she'll be on the bottom afore you know it. River's full o' snags here an' they cain't be seen in the dark.' There was a triumphant note in Sam's voice.

Mason digested the news silently.

'Is he right, Mason?' It was Joe Lascar who asked the question.

'That depends,' Mason said slowly, his eyes on Sam. 'I've heard o' you, Pepper. Best river man on the Mississippi so they say. You knows this ol' river like the back o' your hand. Moon'll be up in a coupla hours. For a man like you, that should be light enough to see by.'

'Can't be done.' Sam was adamant.

'You'd better change your mind, ol' man, or in two hours' time one of these 'ere boys dies or mebbe the girl.'

'You can't do that!'

'Wrong, ol' man. Fella wi' the gun can always do jus' what he wants. There's been a posse doggin' us for a few days; be here sometime tomorrow, I reckon, an' by then I wanna be long gone.'

'You killed our engineer. Can't run a riverboat wi'out an engineer.'

'I use ta work the river one time. Don' take much to keep the boilers stoked. Big boy here can do that, if'n he's still alive. Now, move!'

They were marched into the forward storage locker that lay just behind the *River Queen*'s boiler room. Twelve foot square and windowless, the storage locker was used to house such cargo as tobacco and whiskey and keep it locked away from thieving hands. It was empty just now save for some broken engine parts and coils of rope.

While Lascar and Crazy Jack used the rope to bind the three at ankle and wrist, Mason looked on, a smirk on his face, a hand gripping Jolene's left upper arm.

When the roping was done and the three were face down on the dusty floor, Mason said, 'You've got until moonrise to think about it, Cap'n. In the meantime the girl stays wi' us.'

'Don' you hurt her, Mason,' Sam warned, craning his head around with difficulty to look at the man.

'Or you'll do what?' A sneer appeared on Mason's face. 'Ain't had me a woman in a coon's age, same goes for Joe an' Crazy Jack, an' Crazy Jack sure do love to cut on women, afterwards,' he said chillingly. 'See you boys in a coupla hours.'

The door slammed shut and the three were left alone in the darkness. Nothing was said as they listened to boots clumping up the outside steps leading to the promenade deck then across the deck to the cabin.

'We gotta do something,' Sam wailed in the darkness.

Ben strained at the ropes holding him, but they had been tied by an expert. He finally gave up and relaxed on the hard floor as best he could.

'Ain't no way out of these damn' ropes,' he grunted breathlessly.

'Save your strength, Ben,' Wes said. 'They'll need to cut us loose to run the *Queen* when she gets moving an' then'll be our best chance to tie up a few loose threads of our own.' He lapsed into silence for a moment, then, 'I'm sure sorry 'bout Solomon, Cap'n. He seemed to take the death of the old folks real hard.'

'He loved Jesse and Corabel. They was like a mother and father to him. Never failed to give him a gift o' some kind whenever we stopped here.' Sam's voice broke with emotion. 'Damn their murdering souls,' he moaned huskily.

'They'll make a mistake, Cap'n, they

allus do an' when that time comes they'll wish they'd never heard o' the *River Queen*,' Ben said grimly.

'But what 'bout Jolene, what'll they do to her?'

'She'll be safe enough for the moment,' Wes declared with as much optimism as he could muster, optimism he did not feel. Mason and his men were outright killers without a speck of remorse or pity in their collective souls. He and Ben had been in some desperate situations before, but none as desperate or hopeless as this one. 'They need our full co-operation an' if'n they hurt Jolene they know they won't get it, so don't worry.'

'You really think so?' Sam's voice brightened a little.

'I really think so,' Wes agreed with more confidence than he felt, glad of the darkness that hid any expression that would betray that confidence.

★ ★ ★

Crazy Jack sprawled in a chair at the end of the long table, leaning forward so that his upper chest and chin rested on the table top. Hat removed, he stared through tangles of long, blond hair that fell about his face at Jolene seated the other end. Mason and Joe Lascar faced each other across the table, glasses of whiskey before them, the air thinly misted with cigar smoke.

They had not taken the trouble to tie her into the seat, believing it would not be necessary. She sat with hands balled into fists resting on the table top, lips compressed into a thin line as she fought to control the panic she felt inside.

Crazy Jack's intense stare unnerved her, but she refused to be intimidated.

Mason and Lascar conversed in low tones until Mason finally looked in her direction and pushed a glass towards her filled with a liberal measure of whiskey.

'Take a drink, girl,' he growled.

'Make a man o' you.' Mason chuckled at his own joke and even Lascar took time out to smile.

'Hell, Mason, don' reckon Crazy Jack'll take it too kindly if'n she was to turn into a man,' he cracked.

Mason glanced at Crazy Jack then back to her.

'Drink up, girl. You might find you need it.'

'I choose who I drink with,' she retorted flatly.

Mason and Lascar eyed each other and made faces in mockery of her words.

'If'n I wus you, Miss High an' Mighty, I'd forget such ideas an' drink.' He leaned towards her and dropped his voice. 'When Crazy Jack get romantic notions, you don' wanna face them stone cold sober.' He sat back up grinning wolfishly as Joe Lascar added, 'An' that's a fact.'

Mason chuckled to himself as he fished a fresh cigar from an inside pocket.

'I'll have one of those, if'n you're offering.' Jolene spoke up suddenly as a desperate plan formed in her mind.

Mason and Lascar eyed her in surprise.

'Knowed me a madam in New Orleans smoked cigars,' Lascar said finally.

'Well I ain't no madam,' Jolene flared.

'I'm sure you ain't,' Mason agreed, amusement glinting in his eyes. 'Your pa know you smoke cigars?'

'I'm of an age to do what I like,' Jolene shot back.

'I bet you are, darlin'.' Mason passed her the cigar and fished a lucifer from his pocket, striking it along the table top.

'I'll light it myself,' she snapped. 'Seen a girl lose her hair letting someone else do the lighting for her.'

Mason shrugged, blew out the match and eyed her with narrowed, thoughtful eyes. She returned his stare boldly yet quaking inside. It was as if he knew she was up to something, but could not figure it out. She herself was starting to have doubts as to the wisdom of her crazy plan, but she was too far into it now to stop.

With a half-smile Mason produced a lucifer and passed it to her. She placed the cigar between her trembling lips and took up the lucifer. Her hand was shaking as she dragged the tiny stick along the table top and it hissed into flaring life.

Heart racing in her breast she grabbed up the glass of whiskey, dropped the lucifer into it igniting the spirit with a dull plop, whereupon she threw the flaming contents of the glass towards Lascar and Mason in a scything arc.

A fan of blue flame shot towards the two men breaking up into burning droplets as it showered over them and splattered across the table top.

The men came to their feet, yelling and shouting, chairs overturning as they beat at the shortlived flames that threatened to become more serious if not dealt with straight away. It was a diversion that gave her the edge she needed.

She leapt up, throwing the cigar from her lips and dived for the small chest where Mason had earlier deposited Wes and Ben's gunbelts. She hauled Wes's Colt Frontier from its holster and turned, thumbing back the hammer.

Mason was already moving towards her, but checked himself, lifting his hands before him as she swung the gun on him.

'I know how to use this an' I will if'n you take one more step,' she cried shrilly, and for the benefit of Lascar and Crazy Jack added, 'I'll kill him if'n you two try anything. Get your hands up where I can see 'em!'

'Do as she says, boys,' Mason ordered. He smiled evilly at her.

'That was good, girl, real good, but what are you gonna do now? That's a mighty heavy gun you're toting an' it's gonna get heavier the longer you hold it. My advice to you is to shoot us now while you got the chance.'

'I might do that, Mason.'

'Naw,' he decided. 'Takes a killer to face a man an' blow his brains out. You ain't a killer. Now we 'uns would've pulled the trigger by now.' Mason smirked at her.

Perspiration dampened her face and palms. The gun in her hand wavered from Mason and with an effort she levelled it at his chest.

'So help me, Mason, I'll kill you,' she cried, but her voice lacked conviction.

Mason's smile broadened.

'You really ain't got the hang o' this girl,' he taunted. 'Never leave a man wi' his guns. Make him shuck his gunbelt first. Ain't that right, Joe?'

'Right enough, Mason.' Lascar was grinning.

Jolene licked dry lips. This was all wrong. She had the upper hand but they were acting as if nothing was wrong, then with a cold chill icing the sweat on her body she realized that Crazy Jack was no longer with them. Mason had kept her occupied allowing him to sneak out of the other door into the darkness beyond.

'Yup, you gotta lot to learn,' Mason sighed, as he caught the direction of her searching eyes. 'What you gonna do now, girl? Ol' Crazy Jack's out there in the dark jus' waiting for you to make a move. You ain't gonna know where he is an' you can't stand there all night pointing that hogleg at us.'

'Put your gunbelts on the table an' I'll take my chances,' she said. Mason chuckled to himself as he and Lascar did her bidding. 'Now move away an' keep your hands where I can see them.'

'She's learning fast,' Mason said to Lascar, as they moved back. 'A mite too late, but she's learning.'

'Better late than never, so they say,' Lascar said.

'Not wi' Crazy Jack on the loose,' Mason responded.

Anger burned the doubt and apprehension from Jolene's mind. They were playing with her, eroding her confidence. Keeping a wary eye on them she removed the pistols from their holsters and tucked them in the waistband of her pants before moving to the door.

'Maybe it's Crazy Jack who'll need to look out,' she said coolly and slipped through the door into the night beyond.

Mason eyed Lascar, a hint of admiration in his eyes.

'Dammit, I think I'm beginning to like that girl.' He reached into his jacket and brought out a Walker Colt grinning wolfishly at Lascar. 'Still a lot to learn though.' He sat down unconcerned at the table and reached for the whiskey bottle. 'Best have another drink. We'll sure as hell hear when Crazy Jack finds her.'

Lascar flopped down grinning.

Jolene's heart was thumping as she crouched at the head of the steps leading down to the main deck. Light fanned up through the square opening illuminating the steps below and she remembered there had been a lighted lamp hanging just above the door of the storage locker.

She looked for any sign of movement, listened for any sound that might betray the presence of Crazy Jack, but there was nothing but the usual night sounds coming from the darkened trees. Water slapped and gurgled softly between the side of the *River Queen* and the bank, adding its song to the night.

Gripping the gun tighter she descended the stairs, nerves taut; heart leaping into her sand-dry mouth at one point when a stair board creaked beneath her foot. To her straining ears the sound was loud enough to be heard back in Mead's Crossing.

At the bottom, she dropped into a crouch and pressed her back against the storage locker wall behind which her pa, Wes and Ben were imprisoned, eyes flickering in all directions.

The overhead lamp made her feel naked and vulnerable. Ahead of her lay ten feet of bare deck before the bales, barrels and crates of the cargo began. Just touched by the fading reach of the light it became a sinister wall of pale light and deep shadows.

She inched along the wall, the gun leaden in her slippery palmed hand, expecting any minute to hear the crash of gunfire and feel the agony of a bullet tearing into the soft flesh of her body.

She reached the door without incident. Surely Crazy Jack must be watching her? Why was he doing nothing but twist and tighten her nerves into painful, taut knots? But then, he was crazy!

Crazy Jack stifled a giggle that rose to his lips. Kneeling in the shadows behind a large barrel he had followed her every move since descending the steps and sidestepping her way towards the door. Using the top of the barrel as a rest for his outstretched arms, he levelled the pistol in a double-handed grip and sighted down the barrel as she turned and faced the door, hand reaching for the handle.

He curbed another of his rising giggles as he aimed the pistol between her shoulder-blades and tightened his finger on the trigger, eyes shining in anticipation.

7

Crazy Jack was vaguely aware of a shadow filling the space between the crates to his right. He was more aware of a flash of silver overhead, but he was totally unprepared for the consequences.

The flash of silver became the blade of a Confederate Army sabre as it passed between his startled eyes and severed both hands from his arms in one keen-edged blow.

Blood sprayed and jetted blackly from the severed stumps of his wrists. There had been no pain and there was still no pain as he sat back on his haunches and raised the bloody stumps before his dazed, disbelieving eyes staring at the mutilation. He remained on his knees for several seconds before stumbling to his feet and venting a long, wailing howl from his lips as he turned and faced the shadow who had dealt the devastating blow.

★ ★ ★

Ben's head snapped up as the door opened and a wedge of light fell across him and Jolene entered.

'Jolene. How in tarnation did you get away from Mason?' Sam demanded in surprise.

'Sure is a sight for sore ol' eyes,' Wes commented.

'My left boot, ma'am,' Ben said urgently. 'There's a knife to cut us loose with.' Ben had just taken to carrying his knife in a boot sheath and was now glad he had.

Jolene nodded, quickly found the knife and was slicing through the ropes holding Ben when the cry came.

'What the damn . . . ?' Ben breathed, feeling an icy tickle between his shoulder-blades as the strange, unnerving cry filled his ears. Jolene paused in cutting Ben's ropes, one hand going to her heart. 'Quickly, ma'am,' Ben said urgently and with a tight-lipped nod Jolene completed her task and Ben stood up shaking the rope coils from his body. She passed Ben the Colt and sawed at the ropes holding Wes.

★ ★ ★

Out on the deck, Crazy Jack's eyeballs bulged in a mixture of fear and superstition that momentarily took his mind from his terrible injuries. He sank to his knees feeling the weakness of death creep over him as his life's fluid soaked darkly into the deck-boards where he knelt.

From between the crates stepped the big form of Solomon, his wet clothes pasted to his body. His left arm hung uselessly at his side, shoulder and side dark with blood. In his right hand he gripped the sabre.

'You shouldn't have done what you did to Massa Jesse an' Miss Corabel,' Solomon rasped, eyes pitiless in his face. 'They never hurt nobody an' you killed 'em.'

'Help me!' Crazy Jack pleaded.

'I'll help you, mister, all the way to damnation's fires,' Solomon said in a terrible voice totally lacking in mercy, and sliced sideways with the sabre. Crazy Jack's head flew from his shoulders in a fountain of night-blackened blood and bounced mushily on the deck as the rest of his body toppled forward.

Booted feet rattled noisily on the wooden stairs leading down from the promenade deck.

'It's that damn Nigra. You didn't kill him, Mason, an' now he's done for Crazy Jack!' Joe Lascar hollered over his shoulder as he and Ike Mason reached the deck, brought out by Crazy Jack's terrible cry.

Lascar skidded to a halt, Ben's Tranter pistol gripped in one hand, and raised the weapon at Solomon who stood looking down at the body at his feet, seemingly unaware of the two until Lascar shouted and only then did he turn his head.

Joe Lascar grinned as he took aim with the pistol. It suddenly struck him that now the money from the Georgetown robbery would be a two-way split and that was just fine with him.

It was the last thought he had as two shots rang out, but they were not from the Tranter, that remained silent as two bullets tore diagonally into Lascar's chest, smashing bone and pulverizing muscle.

Lascar's body jerked. The man went down on one knee, coughing bright arterial blood from his lips. The Tranter fell from his hand and slithered across the deck as he toppled sideways and lay still.

Ben rose to his feet before the wall of cotton bales where his dive through the open door and forward roll had brought him.

'Drop it, Mason, or I'll drop you!' Wes shouted, as Mason brought up his gun to fire at Ben. 'I'll get you afore you pull the trigger.'

To Mason, Wes sounded grimly confident and the bearded, robber-killer dropped the gun and raised his hands, turning towards Wes.

'Ease up on the triggers, gents,' Mason called, as Wes and Ben strode grimly forward. 'I'll do a deal wi' you. Half the money from the Georgetown robbery. Fifteen thousand dollars is yours if'n you let me go.'

'Is that all?' Wes raised his eyebrows.

'Make it twenty.'

'Why not the lot?' Ben prompted. 'Shoot you an' we get to keep all the money.'

Mason licked his lips, eyes flickering from one to the other.

'You wouldn't do that to me?' He sounded anxious.

'No, we wouldn't. The money goes back to where it came from an' the law gets you,' Wes said. 'Like you, Mason, we like to clear up loose ends. Get some rope, Ben, an' we'll get this ranny bedded down for the night.'

By the time Mason had been hogtied to their satisfaction, Sam and Jolene had managed to get Solomon into the promenade lounge and seated in a chair. Solomon's eyes flickered in their direction as Wes and Ben came in.

'That fella won't be giving us no more trouble tonight,' Ben declared, and then grimaced at the sight of the wound Jolene had exposed in cutting away Solomon's shirt. Mason's bullet had creased Solomon's left upper chest in a deep, bloody gouge and ripped the muscle and flesh on the inside of his left upper arm. Neither wound was life threatening, but Solomon had lost a lot of blood and a greyish pallor infused the dark pigmentation of his face.

'Might not seem it now, Solomon, but you're one lucky fella,' Wes said. 'Coupla inches more to the right and . . . ' He didn't need to finish the sentence.

'I had to do it. He killed Massa Jesse an' Miss Corabel. He had a bead on Miss Jolene. He wus gonna gun her down. I hadda stop him.' There was a pleading note in Solomon's voice as though he expected not to be believed.

'You done right, Solomon,' West asserted and Ben nodded vigorously at his side. 'The man was an evil killer.'

'Will you boys stop a-jawing an' let me get this wound dressed?' Jolene said crossly.

'Yes, ma'am,' Ben boomed out, raising his hands in a gesture of peace, a big grin on his face, stepping back.

Sam collected four glasses from a cabinet and the three gathered at the far end of the table leaving Jolene to clean and dress Solomon's wound in peace.

The sabre Solomon had used on Crazy Jack lay stained with blood on the table top.

'How'd he come by that?' Wes asked, as Sam splashed whiskey into the glasses.

'It was Jesse's. He was given it by

a confederate officer he helped in the war. Jesse gave it to Solomon 'bout two years ago. They wus allus giving him something an' Solomon, he polished and honed that sabre 'til it shone an' was sharp enough to shave with.' Sam lifted the bottle against the light, a scowl on his face. 'Damned thieves. Ain't left much,' he growled.

'Sure saved our bacon tonight,' Wes pointed out soberly.

'If'n Mason hadn't been so sure o' himself, then mebbe things would turned out a mite differently. As it was, wi' Solomon wounded but still alive, he jus' bided his time an' waited for the right moment,' Sam praised, handing Solomon a glass.

'I'll drink to that,' Ben said.

'How 'bout you, girl?' Sam gave Jolene a sly glance.

Jolene paused in her doctoring and gave her father a sheepish look.

'If'n you don't mind, Pa, I think I'll pass on that offer this time around,' she replied, much to the amusement of Wes and Ben and drawing a tired smile from Solomon.

Later, with Solomon bandaged up and asleep in his bunk, Jolene brewed coffee and dished it out in battered tin mugs.

The moon had come up turning the river into a glittering silver band. It frosted the deck of the *River Queen* in its cold light and filled the nearby forest with shafts of white.

The four had taken their coffee out on to the deck.

'What we gonna do wi' that ranny Mason?' Sam wanted to know. 'Still a-ways to Harper's Ferry, if'n you got it in mind to turn him over to the law there?'

'No need for that, Sam. Remember what Mason said 'bout a posse being close on his heels? Reckon if'n we hang on here they'll come to us an' they can have Mason.'

The posse of ten men came mid-morning. Everyone had managed to grab a little sleep, and Wes and Ben had just finished swabbing down the deck where Crazy Jack had died, when the posse rode out of the trees.

The bodies of Crazy Jack and Joe Lascar now lay side by side on the riverbank, covered with old blankets plus a bloodstained gunny sack containing Crazy Jack's head and hands.

'Got hissel caught in the paddle,' Wes explained.

The leader of the posse made no comment. He was only too pleased to get the money back and Ike Mason under arrest.

'Reckon there'll be a reward for these rannies,' he called out, as Mason was bundled on to a spare horse.

'Send it to Sam Pepper, Mead's Crossing,' Wes called back.

★ ★ ★

The following two days passed uneventfully. Solomon was up and about, but with his arm in a sling he could do little but supervise Ben as the latter tended the boiler. It was on the third day that the river widened dramatically and by midday a series of small, leafy islands appeared ahead.

'They call 'em Reefs,' Sam informed Wes as the two occupied the pilothouse. 'Ain't no problem as long as we keep to the centre channel. Take 'bout a day to clear 'em. It was a place to be feared in the ol' days.' Sam gave a chuckle. 'It was where the river pirates waited. Cabot Longjohn, Deke Trist.' He shook his head, a wistful smile on his leathery features. It was almost as if he admired the men he spoke of, but time has a habit of softening the memories about men who were hardened killers and thieves at the time.

'What 'bout now?' Wes asked.

'Like the riverboats, Wes, the days of the river pirates are all but over. Ain't much to worry 'bout now from these islands but grounding yourself on one in the dark. We'll fetch up on one afore nightfall an' tie up for the night.

Give us a chance to cut wood.'

As the afternoon progressed, the islands grew thicker and as the sun began its descent in the west, Sam brought the *River Queen* to rest in the lee of a small, thickly wooded island. Here Sam had Wes leapt ashore and tied the boat with a single mooring line from the blunt prow to a convenient tree stump.

While Jolene prepared a meal, Wes and Ben went ashore and cut logs to feed the hungry fires of the boiler. By the time they had finished and the meal was ready the sun had almost set and a thin mist was forming over the water. The mist had thickened considerably by the time the meal was over.

It hung around the outside lamps, diffusing the glow, catching and containing the light in a soft, yellow ball, wrapping the *River Queen* in a grey, damp shroud.

Sam had just finished recounting one of his many tales when a thin, haunting wail penetrated the walls of the upper lounge.

'What in tarnation?' Sam muttered as the sound faded and they exchanged puzzled glances.

The sound was repeated.

'Mebbe it's ghosts, Cap'n Sam,' Solomon ventured uneasily. 'I hear'd tell that these islands is haunted on account o' the folks that died hereabouts; murdered by the pirates.' Solomon nodded and rolled his eyes.

'Rubbish, Solomon,' Sam cried scathingly, getting up.

'You ain't going out there, Cap'n?' Superstitious fear creaked in Solomon's voice.

'Well I ain't sitting here wondering,' Sam replied, crossing to a cupboard and taking out his old scattergun and a handful of cartridges. 'Could be Seminoles looking for easy pickings. If'n it is, then they're gonna be picking buckshot outa their red hides. You boys coming?'

'You're not leaving me out,' Jolene

said stoutly, following them to the door and, after a moment's consideration, Solomon decided to join them.

'Came from the open river I reckon,' Sam declared, as they descended to the lower deck and moved to the outer rail, peering into the mist.

The strange sound was repeated a third time. It came from the open water away from the island. It made the hairs on the back of Wes's neck stand up and he drew his Colt as he stood at the rail.

'Over there!' Ben pointed straight ahead. There was a strange, pink tinge suffusing the mist. Hardly anything to begin with, but as they watched, it grew stronger changing from pink to a dull, shapeless red. Then against the red the dark form of a man began to take shape.

'Lordy, Lordy!' Solomon moaned softly. 'The Devil's a-coming to take our souls.'

The strangeness of the apparition coupled with Solomon's obvious dread transmitted itself to the others.

'Damned if'n I ain't never seen the like o' that afore,' Ben declared softly, gripping his gun tighter.

The image sharpened as it came nearer and Ben felt more than relief when he saw it was a man. He stood at the front of a solid looking raft. Behind him the red glow came from a metal brazier filled with glowing ash. Behind that, at the rear of the raft, stood a second man propelling the craft with a long pole. The latter stopped his task at a command from the first man and the raft drifted.

'I knowed it wus you, Pepper, soon as I clapped eyes on that pile of ol' timber you call a riverboat,' the man called out, placing hands on hips.

'Who are you, mister?' Sam called out.

'Dammit, Pepper, don't you recognize me?' The man bent down and lifted aloft a lantern that was behind his feet. The misty light lit up the strong, handsome features of a man with dark hair tumbling from beneath his hat and a thick moustache curving down past the edges of a wide, grinning mouth. 'You should do, you ol' river rat, seeing as how you put me away some ten years ago.'

'Gator Riggs!' The name exploded from Sam's lips in utter disbelief.

'That's it, ol' man. I allus said I'd come back for you an' I'm a man who keeps his word.'

As he spoke, two more rafts drifted out of the mist to join him. Though unlit, the light from Riggs's brazier was enough to show that each raft carried four heavily armed men. As they looked, one of the men raised something to his lips and blew, filling the air with the unearthly wail.

'How'd you like my siren, Pepper?' Riggs called out.

'What do you want, Riggs?'

'You, ol' man. I got me ten years o' prison hate to get rid of an' I aim to take it outa your miserable hide!'

'Jus' in case it ain't come to your

attention, Riggs, we're all armed while you an' your water scum ain't in a position to move outa the way o' flying lead,' Sam shouted.

Riggs laughed, apparently unconcerned at the thought.

'You might miss,' he suggested mildly.

'Don' need to aim wi' this smokepole, jus' pull the trigger an' the fish'll be feeding on you an your boys for days.'

'Thought a man was supposed to get wiser as he gets older, Pepper? Well you sure ain't.'

Sam scowled angrily at Riggs.

'What in thunder are you jawing 'bout, Riggs?'

'It ain't the boys you can see you gotta worry, 'bout. Ain't that right, Flynn?' Riggs raised his voice.

'Right 'nough, Gator.' An amused voice came from behind and all turned in dismay. Wes felt sick with disgust at himself. He had fallen for the oldest trick in the book. Riggs had used himself as a decoy to allow more of his men to approach from behind. ' 'Preciate you boys drop the guns,' Flynn drawled and, accompanied as he was by six others, rifles pointing, Wes and the others had little choice but obey. 'Come aboard, Gator, you got yoursel' a riverboat!'

8

'Is this little Jolene?' There was admiration in Riggs's voice. 'Hell, Pepper, I guess you managed to do somethin' right. Hello, darlin'.' Aboard the *River Queen* Riggs paused before Jolene.

'I ain't your darlin',' Jolene returned frostily.

Gator Riggs took a step back. In his mid-forties, he was still a handsome man, slim-waisted with a smile and flashing eye that had melted many a female heart.

'I see you got your pa's bad temper,' he said, his words bringing a round of laughter from his men who circled the group on the lower deck. 'Sure would be a challenge taming you.'

'Leave her alone, Riggs.' Sam pushed himself between Riggs and Jolene. 'I'm the one you want, leave her and the others alone.'

The smile slipped from Riggs's face to reveal a cold, hard look.

'Ten years in lousy prison because of you, Pepper. Ten years dreaming of the day I'd meet up wi' you agin. Ten years hoping and praying you hadn't died and robbed me o' the pleasure of this moment.' He stuck his face close to Sam's. 'Sure I want you, Pepper. Now I've got you an' you've got ten years of suffering to catch up with.' He straightened and turned his head. 'Get this pile o' logs moving, Flynn.'

'Moving! You'll sink us all if'n you start moving in this fog,' Sam yelped in alarm and the smile returned to Riggs's face.

'Believe me, Pepper, that's the least of your troubles. But you've no need to worry: Flynn knows riverboats an' he knows this 'ere part of the river better'n anyone else.'

A few moments later, mooring line released, the *River Queen* moved away from the island, paddle turning at half speed and disappeared into the fog with Flynn at the wheel and two other men tending the boiler.

Riggs was true to his boast; Flynn knew his job and while islands loomed out of the mist on either side, none appeared ahead to impede their progress. It was an hour later that Flynn brought the *River Queen* to a halt in a small bay, running it alongside a narrow, stilt-legged jetty that marched out into the bay. Then, as soon as the *River Queen* was moored fore and aft, the group was marched off inland through the trees.

It was not a long journey, perhaps ten minutes, before they arrived at their destination which consisted of a circle of crude huts ringing a large fire. The fire served a number of purposes; it provided light, heat and a means to cook food.

A number of raggedly clad individuals watched silently as the victorious river pirates led their prisoners in. The four men were thrown into a hut with a pair of armed guards on the door. Jolene was taken away to another part of the camp, Sam calling after her through a tiny barred window in the door of the hut. It was the only opening to the outside the hut had.

'Damn that Riggs,' he cried vehemently, turning away from the window. With Sam no longer blocking the window, the orange glow from the fire fell across the faces of Wes and Ben.

'I'm inclined to agree wi' you,' Ben said sullenly. 'I'm sure starting to get real upset the way folks keep locking us up.' Wes eyed his big companion. He recognized the tone in the big man's voice. Ben was slow to anger, but once the fires were kindled it was the devil's own job to keep them under control. Wes tended to look upon Ben as a volcano. Once he erupted there was no way to stop him until the fires cooled.

'What's the story about you and Riggs, Sam?' Wes asked, keen to get Ben's mind away from his growing anger.

'Ain't much to tell really,' Sam said wearily. 'Riggs an' his boys were causing a whole heap o' trouble to boats passing through the Reefs. He was killing off trade which was already on the decline, so us riverboat captains an' owners got together an' hired us a bunch o' wild boys, boys good wi' their guns an' willing to use them. Riggs hadda reward o' two thousand dollars on his head so we upped it to five an' found us ten men willing to take on Riggs an' his crew.' Sam paused and stared anxiously through the tiny barred window. 'I sure do hope Jolene's all right.'

'She'll be fine,' Wes asserted. 'Riggs don't seem to be in a hurry to do anything. So what happened to Riggs?'

'We decided to use one riverboat to take our hired gunmen in to where Riggs had his hideout.'

'You an' the *River Queen*,' Wes said with a nod.

'The plan, such as it was, worked well. We took Riggs an' his boys by surprise, damn near wiped out his whole camp. Took Riggs himself prisoner an' delivered him to the law. He got ten years an' swore when he got out he'd come looking for me. Guess I shoulda paid more attention to that part.'

'Don't blame yourself, Cap'n. If'n Ben an' I took notice of the number o' rannies who said they come an' get us when they got outa the hoosegow we'd be permanently looking over our shoulders.'

'If'n you don' mind me saying, Wes, that ain't much comfort to me now.'

While Sam had been telling his story, Ben had been listening and moving around the interior of the hut testing the solidity of the walls. Now, as silence settled between the two men, he spoke up.

'Wood's rotten in a coupla places. Could break outa here an' make a run for the trees.'

'You're forgetting Jolene. Riggs would still have her. Just hold your horses, big fella, our chance will come. Rest up now, save your energy for when we need it, both of you.'

★ ★ ★

'Well, good morning, boys, an' how are we this fine day?' The genial greeting came from a ponchoshrouded Riggs as the door of the hut was kicked open and Riggs stood in the doorway, the strong, early morning light streaming past him to prod at sleepy eyes. The air was chill and raw and without the benefit of a blanket or poncho it bit spitefully into the bones of the four as they arose stiffly to their feet.

'What do you want, Riggs, damn your hide?' Sam spat out.

'Brought you a visitor,' Riggs replied, and stood aside as Jolene was thrust unceremoniously into the hut.

'Pa!' She ran forward and hugged the old man.

'Are you all right, girl?'

'Yes, Pa.'

'But that's only temporary,' Riggs said. 'Bin a long time since I had me a good woman. Mebbe you'd like to watch, aye, ol' man?'

'You dirty scum,' Sam raved. 'It's me you want. Me who had you put behind bars. Do what you want wi' me, but let my daughter go an' these boys. They ain't part of our time.'

'Wrong, ol' man. Letting you watch them die is a sweet bonus to my revenge on you. Letting you watch as all my boys get a turn to party wi' your bitch daughter is gonna be real nectar to me.' Riggs laughed, the sound covering the angry rumble in Ben's throat.

Wes gave his partner an anxious look. The big, silver-haired man's face was set and grim; the volcano was about to explode.

Ben threw himself at Riggs, fist swinging.

Riggs flew backwards through the doorway taking with him one of the two guards. The other guard could only gape as the tawny form of Ben dived on Riggs.

Inside the hut Wes muttered 'Damn!' under his breath and launched himself at the startled guard. It was a no-win situation for already men were running to the aid of their fallen boss.

For a few moments chaos reigned before rifle butts were used to great effect, clubbing Ben to the ground. Wes gave in more easily, raising his hands as a ring of armed hard-faced men surrounded him.

Flynn helped a dazed Riggs to his feet. Riggs kicked the unconscious Ben hard in the ribs before turning angry eyes on Sam who stood in the doorway with his arms protectively around Jolene.

'Looks like we've got our first candidate for the pit, ol' man. You can tell 'im the good news when he comes around.'

Sam's face whitened.

'You mean it's still alive?'

Riggs grinned wolfishly.

137

'Ten years bigger an' a whole lot meaner. Seeing as how your man likes a fight, now he's gonna get one. Get 'em locked up 'til it's time,' Riggs barked out the last, turning away.

'You can't do it, Riggs, it ain't right. For God's sake!' Sam shouted after him hoarsely, as they were bundled back into the hut. 'It ain't right,' Sam moaned brokenly as the door was slammed and the wooden bar dropped into position to hold it shut.

Ben groaned as consciousness returned. Wes and Solomon helped him into a sitting position against the back wall and Wes crouched before him shaking his head in a resigned manner.

'One of these days, big fella,' he said.

Ben grinned wryly. 'Seemed like a good idea at the time,' Ben replied unrepentantly. 'Anyone seen my hat?'

'I got it, Ben.' Solomon handed him his hat and Ben winced as he put it on, as bruised side muscles stretched.

A gloomy light now filled the hut,

pouring in through cracks made by the warped timbers of the walls.

'Could be that that day's come,' Sam spoke up gloomily from where he stood by the door.

Wes eased himself into a sitting position beside Ben and eyed Sam.

'What's this pit, Riggs spoke 'bout, Sam?'

'You ever wondered 'bout the name Riggs has got, Gator Riggs?'

Wes shrugged. 'Suppose you tell us.'

'Gator, short for alligator an' the Mississippi alligator is one mean reptile to get on the wrong side of. Most are found in the swamps below Natchez, but there are a few colonies upriver an here on the Reefs is one such colony. Riggs got the name Gator because . . . '

'He thinks he's as mean as one,' Ben cut in.

'Because he kept one as a pet,' Sam replied. 'Had a special pit dug an' the story goes that if'n anyone crossed him they'd end up in the pit with an alligator for company an' there ain't but one way that meeting would end.'

Jolene gave a gasp and Wes felt a chill wash over his body.

'An' that's what he's got in store for us,' Wes said flatly, making a statement rather than asking a question.

'Wi' Ben as the first victim.' Sam's head dropped. 'I'm sorry, boys, it's all my fault.'

'Now don' go blaming yourself, Cap'n,' Wes spoke up, coming to his feet.

'He's right, Pa. You had no way o' knowing that Riggs was back,' Jolene said, putting an arm across the old man's bowed shoulders.

'I can take care o' myself, Cap'n.' Ben came to his feet, grimacing as his bruised body protested sharply at the movement. 'I once fought a grizzly barehanded an' I'm still here.'

'Gators ain't grizzlies,' Sam rapped out savagely, lifting his head and fixing Ben with a hard stare. 'What d'yer

140

know 'bout 'em, boy?'

Ben shrugged. 'Can't say I'm much acquainted.'

'Then let me tell you: one end is all teeth an' the other is all tail an' in between is two hundred pounds o' hungry body. It can be anything from eight to fifteen feet long an' when it sees you it'll have only one thing on its mind an' a jawful o' teeth to do it with. It can also use its tail. One swipe from that an' you'll think you've been kicked by a mule.'

'Sounds like a woman I once knew,' Ben murmured.

'Dammit, boy, it ain't no joking matter,' Sam raged. 'It's a killing machine with armour for a hide an' death in its soul.'

'Sounds like the hell of a critter,' Ben muttered.

'Hell just 'bout sums it up,' Sam agreed tiredly.

They had little time for further talk as the door was flung open a second time and they were motioned out by

141

men with guns and marched across the camp to where Riggs and Flynn were waiting on the edge of a deep, steep-sided pit some thirty feet across and eight feet deep. The bottom of the pit was filled with dirty water.

It seemed that the entire camp had turned out to join Riggs and Flynn and the pit was ringed with men waiting in silent anticipation.

'Good morning again, Sam Pepper an' Miss Jolene. Glad you an' your boys could make it.' Riggs chuckled at his own joke and his eyes fell on Ben. 'I'm especially glad you could make it, big boy.' He fingered a swollen discoloration on his jaw as he stared at Ben. The latter smiled.

'Walk into something, Riggs?' he asked genially.

'Not as much as you're 'bout to walk into,' Riggs replied, and Ben gave an indignant shout as his hat was snatched from his head. 'Lose the shirt!' Riggs ordered. 'Or I'll have it ripped off your back.'

With a shrug Ben removed his shirt.

'Mighty kind of you to look after them for me. I'll be needing 'em later.'

'I like a man with a sense of humour,' Riggs acknowledged. 'It makes his pleas for mercy so much sweeter.' Riggs inclined his head and three men moved toward Ben, guns aimed at him, but the big man held his ground, even took a step forward, a dangerous smile on his face. It made the approaching three pause and eye Riggs nervously.

Riggs gave a laugh at Ben's show of bravado.

'How 'bout you come here and throw me in?' Ben invited.

'Spirit as well as a sense of humour, how wonderful,' Riggs complimented, as he drew his handgun and thumbed back the hammer.

'Sure will spoil the fun if'n you shoot me,' Ben pointed out.

'I have no intention of shooting you, big boy.' He swung the gun down until the barrel rested against the side of

Wes's right knee. 'Ever seen a man wi' his knees blown off? Sure is painful.'

'Kinda makes dancing a mite difficult too,' Ben replied flatly.

'That's a fact. He's first; the girl's next. It's up to you.'

'You make it awfully hard for a fella to argue with,' Ben replied, turned and slithered down the steep bank into the waist-deep, muddy water below.

'A wise decision. I'm sure you'll die to regret it,' Riggs called, holstering the gun. 'By the way I'll give you a tip: the power of a gator's jaw is all in the downward snap. Catch it by the snout afore it opens its mouth an' it won't be able to.'

'You're all heart,' Ben shouted back.

'Ain't I just,' Riggs agreed. 'OK, boys, let 'im loose,' he called and all eyes were drawn to a point on the far side where four men with ropes proceeded to drag a long, coffin-like box from the bushes. When the end of the box was over the edge of the pit the front was hauled up out of its runners and the men scattered.

Something moved within, venting an angry hissing sound.

A greenish-grey snout appeared then a head with big, raised eyes. Thick, stumpy, clawed legs dragged a fat, heavy reptilian body forward and it slithered down the bank, its own weight taking it in an undignified slide into the water.

The last part of it to emerge from the box was its long, tapering tail that thrashed wildly back and forth as the creature hit sending ripples racing towards Ben.

He felt his stomach churn in panic at his first sight of an alligator as it glided lazily towards him, the eyes in the flat, arrow-shaped head fixed intently on him. Only the barest minimum of the creature showed above water; eyes, snout, part of the scaly back and tip of the tail.

Ben felt his muscles tense as the distance between them closed, then at the last moment it turned and sped back the way it had come.

It was only a brief reprise!

Sweat and water combined on Ben's body. He had never seen anything like it before and genuine fear rippled through him.

The alligator reached the far side of the pit opposite Ben and with a flick of its tail, turned and came back towards him once again.

Ben braced himself and almost shouted his fear as the alligator's mouth opened to show a gaping pink maw lined with backward angled, razor-sharp teeth and he knew that this time it would not turn away. This time it was coming in for the kill!

9

Jolene gave a scream that she tried to stifle with her hands. Sam, ashen faced, turned away. Wes, unable to look away stared horror-struck at the scene unfolding before him while Solomon sank to his knees, hands clasped together, lips moving in a silent prayer.

All that Ben could see was the huge, tooth-fringed mouth gaping wide as it sped rapidly towards him. He waited until the very last moment then threw himself desperately to one side.

The creature rose out of the water in a shower of flying spray, jaws snapping audibly shut, narrowly missing the naked flesh of the big man as he cannoned against the bank and felt his feet slide out from under him. In an effort to save himself he twisted around and dug his fingers into the slippery bank.

At the same time the alligator turned away and its scything tail lashed against Ben's shoulders, smashing him face forward against the bank and driving the breath from his body. Spitting and retching muddy water from his mouth, Ben regained his feet and turned to face his predatory opponent.

Ben evaded the murderous mouth for a second time and as the reptile turned, he launched himself on to its back and wrapped his arms tightly around its thick neck and held on.

The unexpected weight caused the creature to flick his body one way and then the other in an effort to dislodge the clinging man.

The men surrounding the pit above whooped their delight at the unexpected turn of events. Riggs shook his head in wonderment and cast Wes an impressed glance.

'Ain't never see'd a man do that afore.'

For Ben the move was not made to impress, it was a desperate attempt to gain himself some time. The drag of the water slowed his evasive tactics and sooner, rather than later, he would not be quick enough and that awful jaw would make deadly contact.

Crossing his ankles beneath the belly of the reptile he hung on.

The alligator rolled over on to its back submerging its clinging host in the muddy water. It rolled and swam, tail thrashing sending up plumes of spray that sparkled in the morning sunlight, completing a circuit of the pit with Ben still holding on, but the big man's grip was loosening.

It dived and rolled snapping its neck from side to side. Ben's shoulders scraped along the bottom stirring up the years of silt until the water was a thick, brown soup.

On the final occasion when the reptile righted itself, Ben released his grip and slid to one side and kicked with his feet to propel himself away.

The alligator, free of its burden, turned in a tight circle, its scything tail passing just above Ben's head as he surfaced.

Three-quarters submerged, the alligator glided towards Ben as the man rose to his feet shaking water from his hair and eyes. As it came closer, Ben grabbed for the closed jaws, one big hand clamping down on the snout holding the jaws closed.

The alligator tried to twist its head free, but Ben's hand was like a vice clamped around its snout. Together the two circled in the centre of the pit as the men above yelled happily at the battle going on below them.

'It's a good move, big boy,' Riggs shouted. 'Jus' depends how long you can hold it.'

Breathing heavily from the exertion, Ben could feel he was tiring rapidly. He had one last desperate move in mind, a move that would drain his strength. If it went wrong he would be at the reptile's mercy.

150

As the creature arched its body in a half-circle position, Ben caught the tail at a section where he could get a firm grip. Man and reptile had moved closer to one side of the pit in their struggles. Breathing harder now and feeling his heart pounding rapidly in his heaving chest, Ben focused his strength into one last, massive effort.

The men above had grown silent now as they waited, wondering what the man was going to do next. Their puzzlement increased as the man began to turn in a circle.

Once, twice, the squirming reptile was spun around in the straight-armed grip Ben held it in. Sucking air into his lungs on the third spin, judging he had gained as much impetus as was possible, Ben raised his mighty arms.

Two hundred pounds of alligator was lifted into the air and with a thrust of his shoulders Ben released his grip and the startled alligator flew into the air and landed with a thump on the edge of the pit, its tail hanging down.

Energy spent Ben sank to his knees in the filthy water and waited. If the alligator turned and fell back into the pit he would not be able to avoid it.

Hissing and snapping with its jaws, the alligator darted forward as the men nearest broke apart in terrified confusion and began to run.

Wes reacted quickly as his two guards were distracted. He tore the rifle from the hands of the man to his left and drove the heel of his left boot hard against the guard's outer right knee. The guard's leg buckled with an ominous crack and the man went down, a scream of agony bubbling from his lips.

As the man went down, Wes drove the wooden stock of the rifle into the second guard's stomach. The man doubled over retching dryly then lost interest in everything as Wes slammed the rifle stock against the side of his head.

There was yelling and shooting all around as the alligator, moving with remarkable speed, charged after the fleeing men.

Wes hauled Solomon to his feet.

'Find a rope an' get Ben outa there,' he shouted, and spun around at the sound of a female scream. Jolene was struggling with Flynn on the edge of the pit, the latter gripping her wrists. Wes ran to her aid, but Jolene resolved the matter by driving her knee up between Flynn's legs.

Flynn gasped, lips stretched in a grimace of pure agony. Bent double and holding himself, Flynn raised his pain-furrowed features.

'Bitch!' he snarled, and half uncurling himself he drew a knife. 'I'm gonna cut you so bad that no man will ever look at you again.'

'Not today, fella,' Wes said, and used a well-placed foot to send Flynn plunging into the pit.

No one was left on this side of the pit, fleeing to the safety of the camp to get away from the enraged alligator. Wes heard shouts and screams from that direction and the crackle of shots.

A bullet buzzed angrily past his right ear as those on the other side of the pit began to stream towards them, shooting wildly. Wes returned their fire sending two of their kind to the ground. The men scattered and dived for cover. Wes grabbed Jolene's hand and ran towards where Solomon, on finding a rope, was hauling Ben up.

The two reached Solomon as Ben appeared over the edge of the pit and sprawled on the ground.

Bullets kicked dust around Wes's and Jolene's feet. Wes replied in kind and was rewarded by seeing another man go down.

Solomon helped the mud-encrusted Ben to his feet as Wes called out, 'How goes it, Ben?'

'I've felt better, but I ain't complaining. Where did that thing go?'

'An' where's Pa?' Jolene wailed.

'Reckon we'll find both in the camp,' Wes responded. 'Let's go see.'

Ben gently shook off Solomon's steadying hand.

'Thank you kindly, Solomon, but I can make it on my own now.'

The group, with Wes in the lead, entered the camp that minutes before had been a welter of noise and was now as silent as the grave. A half-dozen bodies were sprawled, unmoving, in the hard-packed dirt of the compound. Two showed terrible injuries indicating that they had been victims of the alligator, the others appeared to have been shot, probably caught in the crossfire as their friends had shot at the creature.

A moan to their left had them all looking as a figure struggled to rise.

'Pa!' Jolene cried, and darted across to the stirring form. The others followed, Wes keeping out a wary eye. Not only had the people gone but so had the alligator.

'I'll be all right, girl,' Sam snapped waspishly as Jolene helped him to his feet. 'Stop your fussing.'

'What happened, Sam?' Wes asked.

'I was chasing after that Riggs varmint an' got knocked down in the rush. Where is everybody?'

'Something we was gonna ask you,' Ben said.

Sam's face cracked in a smile as he eyed Ben.

'Lordy, Ben, but that was something. Never seen a man lift a full-grown gator afore, least of all throw it.'

'It's sure something I don' intend to make a habit of,' Ben replied with a wry smile.

'Let's get back to the *River Queen* while the going's good,' Wes cut in.

'Good idea,' Sam declared. 'Wherever these boys have gone they ain't gonna stay away forever.'

They moved cautiously across the camp and were level with the fire that still burned when Riggs followed by three others appeared from a hut to their right.

'Hold it right there, folks, I ain't finished wi' you yet,' he called triumphantly, a smile on his face.

'Nor me wi' you, Riggs,' Ben countered harshly, and grabbed up a burning brand from the fire. 'Down!' he directed at Wes.

'Hit the ground!' Wes yelled and threw himself to the right as Ben hurled the brand, a three-foot section of thick branch at Riggs.

Riggs ducked, finger jerking on the trigger at the same time, but his aim was way off for Ben had dived to the left on releasing the burning branch.

Wes rolled over on to his stomach and fired his own rifle as the section of burning branch hit the veranda fronting the hut in a shower of sparks and bounced through the open door.

Wes's shot, more by luck than judgement, winged a man to Riggs's right, sending the man to his knees, blood pumping from a shattered shoulder.

With a curse, Riggs turned his rifle on Wes and the bullet fountained dirt where Wes would have been had he not continued his roll.

Ben rolled on his back, snatched a second brand from the fire and threw it at Riggs. It hit the dirt just in front of Riggs causing the man to leap back before he could get a second shot at Wes. The latter had now come up on a knee and a foot, the rifle bucking in his grip as he levered a series of rapid shots at Riggs and his men.

A second man buckled as a bullet smashed through his chest and emerged through his back carrying blood and splintered vertebrae.

The third man didn't bother to return Wes's fire, instead he turned and bolted for the trees leaving Riggs on his own.

Riggs fired at Wes, narrowly missing the cowboy.

Grim-faced, Wes sighted on Riggs and pulled the trigger only to have the hammer fall on an empty chamber; the rifle had run out of rounds.

The snarl on Riggs's face became a smile as Wes levered and pulled two more times with the same effect.

'Your luck's jus' run out, cowboy,' he taunted, as he came to his feet and circled around to face Wes directly and keep the others in view. Over his right shoulder black smoke was beginning to billow from the door and windows of the hut that Ben's flaming branch had bounced into. If he saw it, Riggs took no notice, his eyes firmly fixed on Wes.

The wounded man was the first to see it. Struggling to rise, his eyes were drawn to the burning hut, flames now licking hungrily around the door-frame, then something else caught his attention, something at ground level that lent urgency and a new-found strength to his floundering.

'Riggs! The gator!' he yelled hoarsely, as he gained his feet.

The others, eyes fixed on Riggs, now looked in time to see the alligator emerge from beneath the hut and run straight towards the man.

Jolene gave a scream. Riggs turned

and his eyes widened in fear. In a frenzy, he fired at the charging reptile to no effect. The brute came on. Its jaws opened wide then clamped shut on Riggs's left leg just below the knee with a terrible crunching noise.

Riggs screamed as his leg was severed at the knee and he fell heavily to the ground. With a shake of its head that tossed the severed limb to one side, the alligator attacked again.

Riggs raised a defensive arm. The terrible jaws of the alligator snapped shut a second time leaving Riggs with a blood-gouting arm stump.

All Wes and the others could do was watch in horror as the alligator went about its gruesome task.

Riggs's struggles and screams became less until the bloodstained jaws clamped on Riggs's head, shattering the skull.

Wes felt his bile rise.

'Let's get outa here,' he said thickly. The others needed no urging.

They reached the *River Queen* without further incident and threw themselves wearily aboard. The cargo appeared to be intact and someone had kept the boiler stoked.

'Reckon Riggs had ideas of his own for the *Queen*,' Sam observed, after retrieving his shotgun that still lay where he had dropped it. Wes and Ben found their weapons and minutes later Sam had the *River Queen* easing backwards away from the jetty. Thick smoke was rising from the island as they cleared the bay and set course for Harper's Ferry on the last leg of their eventful journey downriver.

★ ★ ★

'This is one trip I ain't never gonna forget,' Sam declared two days later as he stood with Ben and Wes outside the pilothouse and watched as below a team of roustabouts unloaded the cargo on the Harper's Ferry waterfront.

'Been sorta interesting,' Ben replied with a grin.

'Interesting! That ain't the half of it.

The only thing is, you boys ain't no nearer finding out what happened to the *Southern Belle* an' all that gold.'

'Trip ain't over yet,' Wes pointed out. 'We still got the journey back an' somehow I think the answer to it all lies in Mead's Crossing and Cord Duval.'

'D'you mean I've been through all that for nothing?' Ben groaned.

'Well, at least you've seen an alligator,' Wes pointed out with an impish grin.

'Give me back grizzlies and mountain lions,' Ben said with feeling.

'We're gonna leave you now, Cap'n. Gotta few enquiries to make wi' the local law. Should be back by nightfall. Come on, big fella.'

Shadows were lengthening across the jetty when Wes and Ben returned.

'So, whadya find out?' Sam demanded impatiently, as the two climbed the companionway to the upper lounge where the old man was waiting.

'Pa, that ain't nice,' Jolene cried.

'Wes an' Ben ain't gotta tell you their business.'

'But they might need some advice?' Sam said hopefully.

'Don' mind Pa. You boys eaten?' Jolene asked.

'Nary a bite all day,' Ben said forlornly, rubbing his stomach.

Jolene nodded. 'Had me a stew cooking on the *Queen*'s boilers most of the day. Should be 'bout done now. Pa, get the plates an' I'll get Solomon to bring it up here.'

'Damn girl,' Sam grumbled, as Jolene vanished out of the far door, but he did her bidding.

'According to the sheriff here, Gabe Deacon's body was found floating in the river a coupla days after he lit out from Cutter's Landing. He'd been beaten pretty bad an' then shot twice.' The meal over, Jolene was filling cups with strong, fragrant coffee when Wes spoke.

'Ain't more'n he deserved,' Sam observed darkly.

'Pa!' Jolene said, shocked.

'Well he tried to burn the *Queen*,' Sam defended.

'Even so,' Jolene began.

'Even so,' Wes cut in. 'He was still carrying a wallet wi' more'n five hundred dollars when they fished him outa the river, meaning that whoever killed him didn't do it for the money.'

'What are you getting at, boy?' Sam demanded.

'That he was killed for what he knew rather than what he had. He was running scared. He had failed to burn the *Queen* so he was running to whoever he worked for looking for protection and that someone lives in Mead's Crossing.'

'Cord Duval,' Sam said.

Wes nodded and sipped his coffee.

'Proving it would be a mite difficult, but that ain't the problem. Deacon was under orders to destroy the *Queen*. He failed and paid the price. No, the problem is why. Allowing that Deacon worked for Duval, why is Duval so anxious to get rid of the *Queen*? He's tried buying her, burning her. He's bought up the entire Mead's Crossing waterfront so you can't dock unless you are prepared to pay an exorbitant mooring fee. Why?'

'Beats me,' Sam said woefully.

'Ten years' time there ain't gonna be a river trade worth having; mebbe less'n that. Sure seems a lotta trouble to go to if'n you're right.'

'That's what's puzzling me,' Wes admitted. 'With all respect to you, Sam, the *Queen*'s business ain't worth anything to Duval, so why go to all this trouble?'

'Well that's as mebbe. What did you find out 'bout the old *Southern Belle* an' all that confederate gold?'

'The official records of the investigation that followed say that she sank with all hands off Butler's Point. Possible cause, sabotage by person or persons unknown sympathetic to the North. It also goes on to say that due to the nature of riverbed in that area further investigation was impossible due to sinkholes. Any more o' that coffee left, Jolene?'

'Sure, Wes.' Jolene jumped to her feet and quickly filled his cup.

'Them sinkholes can drop a hundred feet or more,' Sam declared with a nod. 'Swallow a boat whole sure 'nough.'

'Thanks.' Wes nodded at Jolene then looked thoughtful. 'Supposing the *Southern Belle* didn't sink, but was only made to look that way and remembering also that in six hours or so it would be dawn, where would you hide a steamboat, Sam?'

'Couldn't, not on this stretch of the river.' Sam was emphatic. ' 'Sides, the only part of the *Southern Belle* found was the paddle an' a steamboat ain't going far wi' out a paddle.'

'No other wreckage?' Wes asked curiously.

'Nothin'!' Sam was adamant.

'Then it was a remarkably clean sinking. Surely if'n it was sunk by sabotage, hit rocks or snags, there would have been more wreckage and bodies. The riverbanks should have been littered.'

'I guess so,' Sam agreed slowly.

'Yet they weren't,' Wes pressed the point. 'An' that, to my mind, makes it all wrong.'

'Surely the investigating officer would have picked up on that point, Wes?' Jolene said.

'Not when you consider that the investigating officer, according to the official records, was a Major Cord Duval.'

'You still ain't come out wi' what you're trying to say here,' Sam cried in frustration.

Wes allowed himself a thin smile.

'I don't think the *Southern Belle* did leave that night or any other night. I think she's still at Mead's Crossing!'

10

The stunned silence that followed Wes's remarkable revelation was suddenly broken by everyone talking at once and Wes flapped his hands to still the noisy babble.

'Heck, Wes, I think you've been out in the sun too long,' Sam cried as the voices faded. Even the normally implacable Ben was taken off guard by his partner's amazing statement.

'Reckon the little fella's been at your sipping whiskey, Cap'n,' Ben drawled, eyeing his partner suspiciously.

Wes smiled, ignoring Ben's remark.

'Tell me about the *Southern Belle*, Sam. What was she like to look at? The one drawing I saw today left me kinda confused.'

'Guess it would,' Sam replied with a nod. 'She weren't no regular steamboat, but an ol' converted flatboat that had been used upriver to transport folk between the settlements before they had roads. She had no upper decks. The boiler was set behind the pilot area wi' just a raised wooden canopy over the two to protect them from the weather. The passengers just found a space on the open deck to sit and got wet if'n it rained. The single smokestack was short by today's standards an' folks using her often got covered in smoke.' Sam smiled at the memory.

'What about size?'

'Fifty foot wi' a beam of twenty, thereabouts.'

'OK, let's put what we know on the table,' Wes began. 'Firstly, Sam, how were you so sure the paddle found that morning was from the *Southern Belle*?'

'That's easy. The *Southern Belle* was blue like the *Queen* here an' the paddle we found was blue.'

'Ain't that real convenient.' There was no hiding the sarcasm in Wes's voice. 'Someone wanted there to be no doubt that the *Southern Belle* sank off Butler's Point.'

'But we heard her leave. Folks further down the river heard her pass by in the fog. Even heard her siren wailing,' Sam said heatedly.

'What they heard, Sam, was a riverboat passing. They were told afterwards that it was the *Southern Belle* an' so believed it. It's my guess the only part of the *Southern Belle* that went down the river that night was the paddle being taken to Butler's Point to give the impression she came to grief there.'

'That's a powerful lot o' guessing,' Sam pointed out. 'So where's she now, if'n she ain't at the bottom of the river?'

'Oh she's at the bottom of the river all right, but in a far more accessible place. With the paddle gone you end up with what she started out as, a flatboat. Sink her in mebbe ten, fifteen foot o' water an' nobody would know.'

170

'What 'bout the smokestack?' Sam cried.

'Removed and dropped in the river.'

'What 'bout the crew an' soldiers that came with the boat?' Ben asked. 'What happened to them?'

Wes shrugged. 'The Confederate Army was in no great shakes on the moral side. Disillusioned, no pay for months, they were deserting in droves. Duval probably paid them to desert, or had them killed. Being the commanding officer at Mead's Crossing he would have known about the gold shipment in advance an' had time to work out a plan.'

'But he wouldn't have known 'bout the fog,' Sam observed.

'Duval's a gambler. I guess he had more'n one ace up his sleeve to get his hands on the gold. The fog was an unexpected turn of luck an' he took full advantage of it.'

'Dammit, Wes, I ain't saying you're wrong an' I ain't saying you're right, but you're getting interesting,' Sam growled.

'Then we'll sweeten the pot a mite. The records office here has a list of officers an' units in the area an' I took particular note of the names of men serving under Duval. Does Private Gabriel Deacon ring a bell? How 'bout a sergeant by the name of Maxwell Hagger, or yet another private, Jubal Tate?' Wes paused, one eyebrow cocked as he waited for a reaction.

Sam eyed him glassily.

'When you get your teeth into something, you don' let go, do you, boy?'

'Hound dog stubborn,' Ben supplied with a grin, eyeing Wes.

'I believe it, same as I'm believing your story better now, but what I can't believe is that he's jus' sitting on the gold an' not doing anything wi' it.'

'He hasn't been, Sam. Duval's a rich man, but he wasn't when he came to Mead's Crossing.'

'He made his money from an inheritance. Some kin o' his died jus' after the war an' left him all his money. Leastways that's how the story goes.'

'Just a cover story. I reckon he's been selling the gold quietly over the years. Nothing big, nothing to stand out an' point the finger. Probably had it melted down an' made into new bars. Ships it down to New Orleans on one of his own boats an' sells it there through an agent.'

Sam slammed a fist down on the table top making plates and cups rattle.

'Dammit, Wes, I'm convinced. So what do we do now?'

'Return to Mead's Crossing an' try an' prove it an' at the same time try an' figure out the connection between the gold an' the *River Queen*.'

'What connection?' Sam barked.

'So far, Duval has tried buying you out, forcing you out an' burning you out, so he won't be looking to welcome you back with open arms. The question again is why?' He eyed each in turn, but all they could do was look blank.

'Sounds to me like the big rancher forcing out the small homesteader,' Ben ventured. 'After all, Sam is the last boat owner at Mead's Crossing an' Duval wants complete control of the waterfront there.'

'Mebbe.' Wes was cautious. 'But I reckon there's something more, though what . . . ?' He shrugged helplessly.

'But why bother stoking up so much trouble for hissel? We ain't no threat to him,' Sam complained.

'Reckon his hand was forced the day that Blake got his hands on that bar of confederate gold,' Wes said thoughtfully. 'Where exactly was the *Southern Belle* moored that night?'

'That's easy 'nough. Right where I moor the *Queen* now. We had one helluva row 'bout it at the time. I had just got back from a trip downriver an' there she was. I tol' Duval he had no right letting her tie up there, but he said there was a war on an' he had commandeered my mooring space for the Confederate Army. I . . . What in tarnation is so funny?' He scowled at Wes who was now grinning broadly.

'That's it, Sam. That's where the *Southern Belle* was sunk. For the past twenty years she's been right underneath the *Queen*!'

'Dammit, Wes. Are you saying I've been sitting on a fortune an' didn't know it?' Sam's expression was almost laughable.

'That's the way of it, Sam,' Wes agreed. 'It was an arrangement that suited Duval until Blake stole a gold bar and opened up a hornets' nest. Duval knows that it's only a matter of time afore the news leaks out an' Mead's Crossing's gonna be filled with official and unofficial treasure seekers. As I see it, Duval needs to move the gold afore that happens an' he can't do it with you there. Once he has control of the waterfront he can close it off to all but his own men and bring the gold up.'

'That's why he's been trying to get rid of you,' Ben broke in.

'And I don't think he's finished trying yet,' Wes said grimly.

'Well wi' what we bin through on this trip, he ain't gonna find that an easy chore,' Sam declared stoutly. 'Ain't got but two stops on the way back. Dynamite for the lumber camp at Snake Cove an' dry goods for Lipman's store at Cutter's Landing.'

'It might be a good idea not to stop until we reach Mead's Crossing, an' wherever you normally stop to take on wood, change it.'

'You think he's gonna try on the river, Wes?' Jolene asked.

'It won't be so easy for him to try anything once we reach Mead's Crossing an' with that in mind, it might be better if'n you stay here until this business is over.'

Jolene's face reddened. Slowly she rose to her feet, hands on hips and fixed Wes with a smouldering look.

Sam looked from one to the other.

'You shouldn't ha' said that, Wes,' he breathed worriedly.

'If'n you think, Wes Hardiman, that after all I've been through that I'm gonna sit here like some good little girl an' wait for you to tell me when it's safe to come out, you've got another think coming!' Her tone was soft to begin with, but it began to rise with the passion she felt and ended in a frosty-voiced challenge.

Ben grinned broadly at his partner's discomfort from the other end of the table, shielding the grin behind a big hand.

'I somehow thought you'd say that, just felt that it was down to me to warn you that the trip back could be a real one-way trip. We are the only ones standing between Duval an' his gold an' he's gonna make damn sure we ain't standing for long.'

'I can take care o' myself,' she said primly.

'Real glad to hear that, ma'am.'

'Folks ain't gonna like me steaming past when they're waiting on goods,' Sam pointed out.

'The object is to stay alive, Sam,' Wes said brutally. 'You can bet your life that Duval has someone here keeping an eye on us at this very minute. He knows the cargo you'll be carrying an' where it's bound. The telegraph is mighty quick in getting information from A to B, so by now Duval knows that too. The only chance we have is to upset Duval's plans by not doing what's expected. Like stopping off at a lumber camp where Duval may have armed men waiting.'

'It makes sense, Pa,' Jolene spoke up for Wes.

'I know it does, girl,' Sam snapped brusquely. He eyed Wes. 'Reckon we can throw a few surprises Duval's way.'

★ ★ ★

Two, uneventful days later found the *River Queen* leaving the Reefs behind on her journey upriver to Mead's Crossing.

178

'Can take twice as long to get back,' Sam informed Wes. 'On the way down we wus running wi' the current, now we gotta fight it. Use up logs twice as damned fast.'

On the morning of the third day, Wes was beginning to wonder if all his theories and guesses about Duval and the gold were on the right track, when Sam called him up to the pilothouse.

'What's up, Sam?'

Sam pointed to the rear. Beyond the glistening paddle blades another riverboat had appeared. Even from this distance Wes could see that the newcomer was much bigger than the *River Queen* and two decks higher. This one had paddles either side and in the early morning sunlight its red and white livery seemed to glow and sparkle like a precious gem on the dark velvet of the river.

'Looks like that trouble you were talking 'bout is here,' Sam cried. 'That there's the *Creole Dancer*, Duval's boat wi' Max Haggar at the wheel.'

'Can we keep ahead of her?'

Sam shook his grizzled head.

'She's got the speed on this ol' gal.'

'What's happening, Pa?' Jolene called as she clambered up the stairs to the pilothouse.

'We got company, girl,' Sam said grimly.

Wes moved to the small section of railed deck behind the pilothouse and waved to Ben, who was helping Solomon keep the *Queen*'s boilers fed with fuel. Ben joined them a few minutes later.

'What d'yer think he'll do, Sam?'

'Well, if'n it was me at the wheel of the *Creole Dancer* I'd ram the *Queen* from behind, smash the paddle to pieces an' she'd be helpless.'

'Then I reckon that's what he's gonna do. How long afore he catches up with us?' Wes looked at Sam.

' 'Bout an' hour, an' he couldn't have picked a better place to do it.'

Wes looked ahead. On the left the riverbank was dense with trees that grew so close together they formed a natural wall. Along the base the water was choppy as it flowed over snags.

To the right, high, grey cliffs rose vertically from the water, neither bank offering a haven to stop; they were trapped.

'River's like this for the next twenty, thirty miles,' Sam declared. 'Damn him. He's got us on the one part of the river where he can do what he likes an' there ain't no one 'bout to see him do it.'

'In that case he's gotta fight on his hands,' Ben vowed. 'I'll allow he'll be short o' crew by the time he takes care of us.'

'Be the other way round, Ben. The *Creole Dancer*'s got the elevation on us. Coupla marksmen on the pilothouse deck an' it's us'll be looking for new crew,' Sam said dismally.

Wes eyed the old man through narrowed eyes. There was already a note of defeat in Sam's voice.

'Are you trying to tell me that an ol'

river man like you ain't still gotta trick or two up your sleeve?' Wes goaded softly.

'Haggar's holding all the aces. The *Creole Dancer* is damn near three times the size of us an' twice as fast. He'll have twenty gunmen, mebbe more, keeping our heads down while he rams us.'

'Ain't size that counts, Cap'n,' Wes snapped back, 'it's what's in here.' He slapped a hand over his heart. 'An' here.' He touched the same hand to his head. 'There's gotta be something we can do? You know the river!'

Sam massaged the back of his neck, frustration painting extra lines on his tanned leather face, then slowly the cloud lifted. He looked around at Wes standing in the doorway of the pilothouse with Ben behind him.

'There might jus' be a way,' he breathed.

'I knew you'd think o' something, Cap'n,' Wes said with a grin.

'You ain't gonna like it,' Sam promised darkly.

'If'n it gives us half a chance, I'm all for it,' Wes replied quickly.

'It means riding through the Jaws, boy.'

On the other side of Sam, Jolene paled and her eyes grew large.

'You can't be serious, Pa? We'll all be killed for sure.'

Wes looked across at her.

'If'n you ain't forgotten, ma'am, that's what's gonna happen to us when the *Creole Dancer* catches up wi' us.'

'A bullet might be better,' she replied tautly.

'Would someone mind tellin' me what the heck these Jaws are?' Ben called out.

'It's some twenty miles of the meanest river you'll ever see. The Indians call it 'The Jaws of Death' an' only a fool would consider that a plan,' she said hotly.

Sam rounded on her.

'Quit callin' your pa a fool, girl. You

had your chance to stay behind, but you voted yoursel' in. Well, there ain't no turning back now,' he concluded roughly, turning back to face Wes and Ben. 'Ahead, the river swings east in a big loop afore it doubles back on itself. The Jaws is a canyon that cuts through yonder bluff on a straight south-north run. Cuts out night on forty miles of river an'll put us a full day ahead of Haggar.'

'Ain't sure I'm following this, Cap'n, but won't Haggar stay on our tail?' Wes asked.

'The Jaws is no ordinary river, Wes. It's narrow; the canyon walls keep the water from spreading out an' that makes the water move faster. Then at one point the canyon floor takes on a slope, ain't much, but then the canyon walls move in to form a mile-long narrows, and that's where it gets its name from. They say the water moves so fast in there that it's apt to tear a boat to pieces,' Sam nodded.

'Have you ever seen it, Cap'n?' Ben

asked, causing Sam's face to crack in a smile.

'Hell, boy, nobody's seen it for the last forty years. The last an' only person who ever rode the Jaws was Cap'n Dawson. He made a bet that he could take his riverboat, the *Natchez Lady*, through the Jaws, an' in the spring of '46 he did just that.' Sam paused.

'An' did he make it?' Wes asked.

'He made it all right, but he was never the same man agin, not right in the head, an' the folks who were there at the time swore that when he entered the Jaws his hair was black, but when he came out it was white.'

'River folk sure do know how to tell a good story,' Ben said with a beam. He swept off his hat. 'Ain't much it can do to my hair.' His humour made them all laugh, easing the tension that had been building somewhat.

'What I'm a-saying, Wes, is that the *Creole Dancer* is too big for the Jaws,' Sam concluded.

'So if'n we make it we'll be a full day ahead of Haggar an' he won't be able to catch us up before we reach Mead's Crossing?'

'That's the truth of it,' Sam replied.

'How long afore we reach the Jaws, Cap'n?' Ben called.

'Reckon 'bout the same time that Hagger catches up wi' us.'

They all looked back. The *Creole Dancer* had increased in size as the gap between them closed.

11

The *Creole Dancer* was an awesome
sight as she rode the wake of the *River
Queen* with less than a hundred yards
separating them. Men were gathered
on the hurricane deck, set above
the promenade deck of the *Creole
Dancer*, their jeering laughter almost
lost amid the rattle and thump of the
two steamboats' engines.

Black smoke billowed from the
towering twin smokestacks of the
Creole Dancer and every now and
again her throaty siren would wail like
distorted laughter in the ears of those
aboard the *River Queen*, mocking and
taunting them.

A sporadic rattle of gunfire tore
into the pilothouse of the *River
Queen* causing Sam to duck down.
On either side of the pilothouse,
Wes and Ben returned the gunfire

scattering the jeering men.

'We ain't gonna make it,' Sam shouted. 'We need more time!'

'How much further, Cap'n?' Wes asked, as a bullet splintered wood just above his head.

'You can see it up ahead,' Sam shouted back, as he rose cautiously to his feet.

Wes moved back and turned his head in the direction Sam was pointing. Up ahead a deep gouge showed in the grey cliffs.

Ben appeared around the front of the pilothouse and joined Wes.

'I got an idea how we might buy that time. C'mon.' He rattled down the stairs to the lower deck before a mystified Wes had time to ask any questions. He threw Sam a puzzled look and followed in Ben's wake.

He found the big man in the storage locker opening one of the cases of dynamite with his knife.

'What's on your mind, Ben?' Wes asked, as Ben set about spiking the ends of half a dozen dynamite sticks and pushing a short length of fuse in each.

'Reckon it's 'bout time we showed ol' Max our teeth.' Ben gathered up the prepared sticks and thrust them carelessly into the pocket of his tan coat. 'I'm gonna see how far I can throw one o' these an' the closer ol' Max gets the more chance I have of getting one on deck. If'n that don't make him back off then I'll eat my hat.'

Wes smiled, appreciating his partner's quick thinking.

'I like it.'

'Gonna need me some covering fire once they figure out what I'm about.'

'You've got it, big fella.'

The two moved to the rear of the *River Queen* and took up a position on the small platform to the left of the great paddle. While Wes knelt down behind the doubtful cover of the rail, Ben lit a long section of fuse that he tossed down on to the deck and used that to light his first stick which he hurled towards the approaching *Creole Dancer* with all his might.

The stick was falling short when it exploded in mid air in a flare of red flame and black smoke.

Guns began blazing from the upper deck of the *Creole Dancer*, splintering the wood of the turning paddle. Wes returned the fire, levering and pulling the trigger of his Winchester in rapid succession.

Ben launched his second dynamite stick on a lower trajectory only to see it hit the water beneath the *Creole Dancer*'s prow and the fuse extinguished before it had time to detonate.

By now, realizing the danger he was in, Haggar slowed the *Creole Dancer* and Ben's third throw fell short, exploding just above the water as the gap between the two boats increased.

'Let's hope that gives the Cap'n the time he needs,' Ben said.

Sam was full of glee when the two joined him and Jolene.

'I like your way o' thinking, Ben. Sure had that varmint Haggar pulling in his horns.'

From the pilothouse of the *Creole Dancer*, Max Haggar watched the distance between the two grow with fury. He hadn't reckoned on this turn of events.

His fury gave way to puzzlement as ahead the *River Queen* was turning across the river. What in damnation was that old fool doing?

It was the thin-faced Reevers, Haggar's first mate, standing next to him who put it into words.

'He's heading for the Jaws, Cap'n!' There was disbelief in the man's voice that was reflected in Haggar's dark eyes. Reeves turned his eyes on Haggar's staring profile. 'He's doing our job for us. That ol' scow'll be smashed to pieces.'

'But if'n he makes it . . . ' Haggar snarled. 'Follow him!'

Reevers's jaw dropped.

'You can't mean it?' he wailed.

Haggar turned on the man.

'You're getting well paid to make sure the *River Queen* never reaches Mead's Crossing, well, now you earn your money.'

'But the Jaws?' A thin beading of sweat sheened Reevers's sallow face.

'If'n Pepper reaches Mead's Crossing, the only payment you'll be getting is a long jail sentence. The stakes are too high to leave anything to chance. That ornery ol' man is jus' likely to make it through an' I wanna be on his tail if'n he does. Now follow him.'

Reevers nodded reluctantly and spun the wheel.

The high canyon walls closed around the *River Queen* as she entered the Jaws. On the promenade deck, Wes and Ben peered apprehensively ahead.

The canyon they had entered was some seventy feet wide; somehow Wes had been expecting something far narrower and this came as a relief.

Keeping to the middle of the channel there was still plenty of room either side of the riverboat. The rhythmic thud of the heavy pistons became magnified in the granite confines, pulsing back at them from the sheer walls.

'Don' seem too bad,' Ben ventured.

'Well it's got twenty miles to get mean in,' Wes replied.

'You sure know how to make a fella rest easy,' Ben returned with a wry smile.

The two moved up to the pilothouse.

'It's like a woman,' Sam expanded. 'Nice an' gentle to begin with, but once she's got you hooked . . . '

'That ain't fair, Pa,' Jolene pouted. 'Men can be jus' the same 'til they get what they want.'

'What this ol' stretch of water's got nobody wants an' that's for sure.' He gave her a scowl. 'How come you know so much 'bout men then, girl?'

Jolene reddened under his gaze much to the amusement of Wes and Ben.

'I ain't saying I do, it's jus' what I heard.'

She was saved any further embarrassment as Ben called out, 'Hey, Cap'n, the *Creole Dancer* is following us!'

They had travelled some 200 yards and looking back the *Creole Dancer* was at the entrance of the canyon.

It was Sam's turn to show disbelief.

'She's too big. Haggar mus' want us real bad.'

'He an' his boss Duval have a lot to lose,' Wes said.

The canyon narrowing gently in and out caused them to lose sight of the *Creole Dancer* every so often.

They had travelled about two miles when Wes noticed a subtle change in the water; it was flowing faster now and the speed of the *River Queen* had risen.

'The good times are over now, boys,' Sam murmured in answer to Wes's unsaid question.

'Anything we can do, Sam?' Wes asked.

'Take the wheel if'n I drop dead from the excitement,' Sam cracked, in an attempt to lighten the unknown danger that lay ahead. But behind the joke lay tension. 'All you can do is hold on, it's apt to get a little rough from now on.'

'Will we make it, Pa?' Jolene sounded scared.

'We'll make it. Got me a score to settle wi' a fancy dresser called Cord Duval an' no trickle o' water's gonna keep me from that.'

As the surging water carried them deeper into the canyon it became more agitated and Wes noticed that the canyon was narrowing. The *River Queen* began to rock back and forth as the water became rippled with angry waves. In an effort to get some sort of control Sam had the engine put into reverse.

For a while it worked but as the flow became faster, the paddle lost its drag effect and Sam was forced to abandon the idea before the engine bearings burnt out.

The roaring hiss of the water became more pronounced as the canyon walls closed in. Ahead, the water began to foam white as the canyon floor shelved. It was only a gentle slope, but the foaming, roaring water poured down the incline at breakneck speed and as it hit boulders on either side, it bellowed and sent fans of spray high into the air.

Wes's heart sprang into his mouth as the blunt prow dipped momentarily beneath the water then reared up in an explosion of flying spray that soon had the decks glistening and Wes and Ben hanging on outside the pilothouse, soaking wet.

With the paddle turning only by the force of the rushing water, Solomon had joined the others, clinging to the rail for support.

The river levelled, but lost none of its impetus. The *River Queen* bucked and dipped like a skittish bronc and the thunder of the rushing torrent increased, pounding into their dazed brains. It tried to push the riverboat against the dripping walls and only the skill of Sam saved them from being smashed to driftwood. Then ahead, through the curtain of spray, loomed a sight that none was prepared for.

Wes felt his throat constrict with fear; Solomon's eyes bulged until it seemed they would pop from their sockets; Ben's thumping heart was firmly lodged in his throat. Jolene screamed and shut her eyes and only Sam remained impassive, bottling the fear that screwed his insides into tight, choking knots.

Ahead, the canyon walls came together leaving just a black, gaping maw of a tunnel the rushing waters disappeared into. They all knew that this was where the river got its name. Before them lay the infamous Jaws of Death and they were being carried helplessly towards them.

Those outside the doubtful protection of the pilothouse threw themselves flat on the deck as the *River Queen* was swept into the dreadful darkness of the tunnel.

The thunder of the rushing water, magnified by the confines of the tunnel, beat into their ears. The *River Queen* grazed one side of the tunnel adding a rasping, splintering screech to the many sounds about them.

Sam managed to ease it away from the wall only to hear the other side grate harshly against the unseen tunnel wall. Ripping, snapping sounds came from the decks below them.

The *River Queen* shuddered and timbers groaned as she ground herself against hidden rocks. To the men hanging on for dear life, the nightmare sounds seemed to indicate that the *River Queen* was being systematically ripped apart by the rocks and water.

A greyness appeared ahead; a speck of light diffused by the eternal mist that filled the tunnel. it grew rapidly in size and suddenly the *River Queen* shot into bright daylight causing all to screw up their eyes. When they finally opened them they found themselves drifting in a wide, deep pool into which the tunnel emptied. The raging torrent that had carried them through lost its impetus in the vast pool and a wonderful silence filled their ears.

The *River Queen* had not come through unscathed. The smokestack had sheered off a foot or two above the level of the pilothouse roof. In places, the rails along the outer edges of the decks had been ripped away, reduced to splintered stumps and the big sternwheel had lost some of its paddles.

In the pilothouse, Sam loosened his knuckle-white grip on the wheel. His face was white, but he managed a strained smile.

'That's one helluva short cut,' he mumbled hoarsely through his whiskers.

'Well done, Cap'n,' Ben boomed out.

'Save your praise, Ben, we still got a'ways to go yet an' the Jaws may have a surprise or two left.'

'I wonder what happened to the *Creole Dancer*?' Wes said.

The *Creole Dancer* had come to a violent, savage end. In the grip of the racing water, there was nothing anyone could do.

Haggar saw the tunnel entrance but was powerless to do anything. He was still in the pilothouse when the *Creole Dancer* entered the tunnel, the entire top deck torn from its mountings in an explosion of splintered boards and shattered rails. The pilothouse flew apart as it was rammed into the cliff wall above the tunnel entrance. Haggar's crushed and shattered body fell into the water amid a cascade of broken timbers and was swept in the wake of the riverboat.

Within the blackness of the tunnel the side paddles were ripped from their mountings and the hurricane deck with its cabins collapsed as the riverboat bounced from side to side, hitting the walls with destructive force. Beneath the flat keel, the boards took a hammering from the submerged boulders that stove ragged holes in the planking.

Before the *Creole Dancer* was halfway through the tunnel, she was breaking up, falling apart, tossing terrified men into the roaring, foaming water to die horribly in the relentless torrent that smashed their bodies on the rocks.

By the time the first pieces of wreckage and shattered, mangled bodies shot from the tunnel into the lagoon, the *River Queen* had gone on to complete its final leg of the journey down the Jaws of Death.

Two hours after entering the canyon river, the *River Queen* emerged into the Mississippi River and headed towards Mead's Crossing.

★ ★ ★

Simpkins, the flabby telegraph man, was sweating profusely as he waited nervously for Cord Duval, seated at his large desk, to read the message that had just come from Cutter's Landing. Flanking the seated man on either side and causing added distress to the telegraph man, stood the silent, darkly clad Lacroix brothers, Henri and Raphael, their dark, emotionless eyes never leaving his face.

Simpkins jumped visibly as, with an oath of rage, Duval crumpled the message into a ball and hurled it across the room before turning fury-bright eyes on the unfortunate man.

'This message never came, is that clear?' he snapped.

'Never came, sir,' Simpkins squeaked. 'Never seen it!' Simpkins responded and Duval smiled faintly.

'Good. Then we understand each other. Now get out and keep your mouth shut or these two gentlemen will be paying you a visit.'

Simpkins nodded his head vigorously, mouth dry.

'No need for that, Mr Duval.' He backed to the door, eyes jumping hotly from one to the other.

'I hope not, Simpkins.'

It was with a sense of profound relief that Simpkins stepped from the room and closed the door in his wake. He had no idea what all the fuss was about, for all the message had said was that the *River Queen* had just passed through Cutter's Landing! He shuddered at the thought of the Lacroix brothers paying a visit. That was one message he would definitely have a bad memory over.

Pulling a dirty linen square from his pocket he mopped his face and fled back to the safety of his office.

Duval stared moodily at the closed door before turning his gaze on Henri Lacroix to his right.

'Get Tate and his two friends in here and let's see if'n we can't turn this situation.'

'You wanted to see us, Mr Duval?' Ten minutes had passed and now Jubal Tate, hat in hand, stood before Duval's desk sandwiched between the stumpy

Harve Baker and taller, leaner Sam Creech.

'We have a problem, gentlemen.' Duval addressed the three while his eyes remained on Tate. Raphael Lacroix remained at Duval's side while Henri had taken up a position by the door. 'It seems that Pepper has somehow evaded Haggar. The man I sent to Cutter's Landing has reported that the *River Queen* is on her way here. I'm looking to you to make sure that she never arrives.'

'Consider it done, Mr Duval,' Tate said. 'Got me a score to settle wi' the one calling hissel Ben Travis.'

'Just make sure that score includes all of them. I'm counting on you, Tate, to complete what Haggar started out to do.'

'Set your mind at rest, Mr Duval, it's as good as done,' Tate bragged. 'Ain't that right, boys?' His head turned back and forth as he eyed his two henchmen.

'Right, 'nough, Jubal,' Harve Baker

growled and Sam Creech nodded his agreement.

After the three had gone Duval lit a cigar and leaned back in his chair, contentment on his face.

'Got a job for you boys.' He waited for Raphael to come forward and Henri to join him before the desk, before continuing. 'Arrange for Simpkins to have an accident. No sense in adding to our problems.'

★ ★ ★

The engine driving the big stern wheel, rattled and wheezed as it turned the wheel against the current, pushing the *River Queen* upriver.

Solomon appeared on the upper deck wiping grease from his hands with a dirty square of rag.

'Ain't good, Cap'n Sam,' he declared mournfully. 'Tha' ol' engine picked itsel' up a heap o' trouble going through the Jaws.'

'Will we make it, Solomon?' It was

Jolene who asked the question.

'Mebbe,' Solomon replied, shrugging his big shoulders.

'We'll make it,' Sam said confidently. 'Can't wait to see the look on Duval's face when we 'uns turn up.'

'When do you think we'll reach Mead's Crossing, Sam?' Wes asked.

'Ain't gonna be much afore nightfall unless we can coax a little more speed outa her.' He eyed Solomon.

'Steam pipes are leaking, Cap'n, an' pressure's way down.'

'Jus' see what you can do, Solomon.'

'Yessum. Do muh best.' Solomon turned away.

'I'll give you a hand, Solomon. Perhaps 'tween us we can manage something,' Ben said encouragingly.

* * *

There had only been one man at the jetty of the lumber camp when Jubal Tate and his two men rode in and he now lay face down in a flat boat, blood pooling beneath his smashed head.

The flat boat was piled high with a double pyramid of rough logs ready for transportation downriver. The flatboat itself was nothing more than a hull with a boiler and stumpy smokestack at the front and engine in the rear to drive the single stern paddle. Between the engine and the boiler the remaining deck space was taken up with the stacked logs.

There were well over 200 logs; tree trunks with their branches removed, the average length of each twenty feet and some a yard in diameter.

Tate had used three bundles of dynamite, each with a length of slow burning fuse attached. The ends of the fuses were in his hands when Harve Baker called out, 'She's a-coming, Jubal!'

Tate looked up as the *River Queen* appeared around a bend a mile downriver.

He watched it for a moment or two, nodded to himself and touched off each fuse with the end of a cigar before clambering back on to the jetty.

'Get them poles, boys an' help me push her out. Once she gets in the current the river'll do the rest an' it's goodbye *River Queen*.'

12

Wes was the first to see it.

'What's that up ahead, Sam?' he called, pointing.

'That's one o' the log boats from the lumber company,' Sam called out through the open pilothouse door. 'Don' worry, son, we ain't gonna hit it,' he added as an afterthought.

That thought had not entered Wes's head. He stared intently at the approaching craft. There was something wrong that he couldn't put his finger on, then it came to him. There was no engine sound coming from it nor any smoke from the smokestack and there was no sign of movement aboard. Looking beyond the stacked logs he could just make out part of the stern paddle. It was turning slowly due only to the drag of the water on its blades as it drifted with the current.

'She's deserted, Sam,' Wes called.

'He's right, Pa!' Jolene had joined him.

Sam stuck his head out of the pilothouse door.

'Musta slipped her moorings. Current's carrying her. She'll fetch up on a sand bar further down. Someone's gonna lose their hide over that.' Sam withdrew his head.

Jolene eyed Wes.

'You thinking Duval might have something to do with that?' she asked.

'I don't know what to think,' Wes replied guardedly, never taking his eyes off the approaching flatboat. 'Them logs could hide a dozen gunmen. Maybe she's not as deserted as she looks.' He dropped his gaze to her. 'Get Ben up here, Jolene. I'd sooner be safe than sorry.'

From a low, tree-capped bluff, Tate and his men watched. They saw Jolene disappear below and return almost immediately with Ben.

'They know somethin's up,' Mason commented.

'But it ain't what they think it is,' Tate breathed, eyes shining with anticipation. He was an expert in handling dynamite, a talent he had expanded on during the war and one he had never forgotten.

'They's getting awful close,' Creech voiced. 'If'n that dynamite don' go off soon they's gonna pass each other an' then it'll be too late.'

Tate eyed him darkly.

'You worry too much, Creech,' he snapped back. All the same he pulled a watch from his pocket and eyed it anxiously. The charges should have gone off by now, throwing a barrier of logs across the river that would force the *River Queen* into the bank to avoid collision. That would make them easy to pick of with rifles and afterwards complete what Gabe Deacon had failed to do; set fire to the *River Queen*.

'You gave it too much fuse,' Creech wailed. 'I know'd it, I damn know'd . . . '

His final words were lost as the flatboat with its cargo of logs exploded.

From the upper deck of the *River Queen*, stunned eyes watched as the forward stack of logs blew apart, lifting into the air on a billowing cushion of black smoke shot through with flickers of orange flame.

A second and third explosion followed a split second later tearing the flatboat apart and sending the second stack of logs cartwheeling into the sky.

Tate's plan was more successful than he ever dared hope. With the thunder of the explosions still echoing in the ears of those aboard the *River Queen*, the first logs began to splash down all around the steamboat, hitting the water and sending up great fans of white spray. Then one came whistling out of the sky and hit the paddle, smashing the blades to pieces. A second dropped upright and passed through the planking of the upper deck, punching a hole in the bottom of the steamboat.

The noise was tremendous as the

logs rained down turning the water around the helpless craft into a white, seething cauldron.

The *River Queen* bucked and rocked as waves, caused by the falling logs, hit the low hull and washed across the lower deck.

The rear section of the promenade deck collapsed, planking reduced to splinters beneath the hail of falling logs, the engine smashed from its supports.

Steam erupted in angry, hissing jets as the pipes running from the boiler to the engine were fractured and broken and still the logs fell, churning up the river and slowly but surely destroying the *River Queen* bit by bit.

Sam abandoned the pilothouse and together with the others cowered in the doubtful safety of the cabin block on the wrecked promenade deck as the stricken *River Queen* listed to port.

A forward section of the promenade deck disappeared in an explosion of snapping, splitting wood as a log slammed down making what remained of the deck shudder beneath them.

Finally the deadly, pulverizing assault from above was over and their ears were filled with the grate and splinter of the logs in the water grinding against the tilting hull of the sinking *River Queen*.

They came gingerly to their feet on the canted deck.

'We's gotta get off, Cap'n Sam,' Solomon wailed. 'Once the water reaches the boiler she's gonna blow for sure.'

They were less than fifty yards from the west bank of the river but the water was littered with logs that rolled together and ground against each other with a sound like muted thunder. If anyone was unlucky enough to get caught between them they'd be mashed to a pulp.

It was not a prospect that appealed to Wes.

An area of relatively clear water was coming up before the next wave of logs came rolling down. Wes pointed.

'Here's our chance,' he called.

Ben removed his hat and stuffed it inside his shirt.

'Follow me,' he boomed and without further ado leapt from the sloping upper deck into the water. The others followed in quick succession and began swimming to the shore. They had covered about half the distance when the boiler on the *River Queen* exploded with a thunderous roar.

Wes looked back in time to see the remains of the upper deck and the pilothouse shatter into pieces around a dark column of smoke.

Burning brands of timber from the boiler's fiery innards shot upwards and outwards in a glowing fountain, each trailing a tail of dark smoke that marked its ascent and then descent.

They fell in the water all around them hissing savagely as the water doused their hot fiery hearts.

As the shattered remains of the *River Queen* slid beneath the turbulent water, jetting gouts of steam and smoke, Wes heard his name called. He snapped his head around. The others had already gained the bank and Ben was pointing urgently upriver.

Something loomed in the corner of Wes's left eye. A huge log bore down on him. Sucking in air Wes dived under the water. The log caught him a glancing blow across the shoulders, spinning him over as he tried to go deeper. From beneath the water he looked up to see the surface now covered with logs trapping him below.

On the bank Ben made as if to enter the water, but Solomon grabbed his arm, sorrow in his big eyes.

'Ain't no use, Mister Ben, he's gone an' you'll be kilt for sure if'n you go after him.'

Ben shook Solomon's grip aside angrily.

'I've gotta find him.'

'He's right, Ben. You'll get crushed if'n you try,' Jolene cried, a sparkle of tears in her eyes.

Ben stared with distraught eyes as the

logs, forming themselves into a long, irregular platform, flowed by, carried by the current.

'Sure is a real shame,' a voice chuckled from behind and they turned to face Jubal Tate and his two cronies. The three, astride their mounts, covered them with rifles.

'Dammit, Tate was you responsible for this?' Sam spoke up.

Tate grinned wolfishly.

'Damn right I was, ol' man. You shoulda died wi' your man. Now, me an' the boys'll have to finish you off.'

'They find our bodies full o' lead an' the law'll come a-looking,' Ben called.

'Don you worry your silver head, big boy, 'cause you'll never know,' Tate jeered nastily. 'Sides, back aways is a nice little swamp. Ain't no one ever gonna find you.' He chuckled again and Baker and Creech joined in. 'Now get rid of the hogleg, big boy, and move straight ahead an' all of you raise your hands real high an' scratch the sky.'

With no other choice, Ben removed

his Tranter from its holster and tossed it aside, it was useless anyway after the soaking it had taken, and led the group forward knowing that any form of defiance on their part would be met by a hail of bullets. He had no intention of giving up his life meekly, but by giving that impression hoped it would make Tate careless.

'Ain't feeling so big now, are you, big boy?' Tate taunted as they walked ahead of the mounted men.

'That's far enough, Tate!' The snapped-out words were accompanied by the ratchet clicking of a hammer being drawn back.

The three riders halted in surprise. The prisoners turned and there was a smile on Ben's face as behind the stopped riders he caught a glimpse of Wes. Clothes torn and dripping, a cut over one eye that painted his left cheek red, the cowboy stood straight and tall, his Colt pointed at Tate's back.

'Keep 'em covered!' Tate barked at Baker and Creech as he turned his horse and faced Wes, rifle pointing down. 'Shoot anyone who moves.' He eyed Wes thoughtfully.

'You're bluffing. That hogleg's wet. It ain't gonna fire.'

Wes smiled. 'Can you be sure o' that, Tate?' he asked mildly.

Tate licked his lips nervously. The man's confidence unsettled him.

'Do somethin', Tate,' Baker called.

'That's right, Tate, do something,' Wes invited. 'What have you got to lose, 'cepting your life, mebbe?'

While this interchange of words had been going on, Ben had edged closer to Creech, who, along with Baker was half turned in his saddle trying to keep an eye on the prisoners and at the same time watch Tate and Wes.

Ben was too far back to make a dive for Creech, but he was within an arm's length of the head of Creech's mount as the germ of a desperate plan formed in his mind.

'Guess I'll have to take that chance then,' Tate called.

At that moment Ben lashed out with his left arm giving the mount a stinging blow on the muzzle.

The animal reacted, whinnying in surprise and pain, rearing up and pawing the air. Taken by total surprise, Creech gave a startled yell and slithered back over the rump of the beast to hit the ground with a bone-jarring thump. He was struggling to rise when the horse's forelegs came back to earth and it lashed out instinctively with its hind legs.

Creech was in the wrong place at the wrong time. An iron-shod hoof caught him full in the face. Bone crunched sickeningly as the man's face was stove in and he flew backwards. He was dead before he hit the ground, front of his skull crushed and splinters of bone driven deep into his brain.

By then Ben was already on the move. The other two animals, alarmed by the cry from Creech's mount, shied away uneasily almost unseating their riders.

Throwing himself forward, Ben slammed a shoulder into the rump of Tate's horse.

The animal bucked and the rifle in Tate's hand roared.

Wes threw himself sideways, but the shot went wide and the next instant Tate's rifle dropped at Ben's feet as the man fought to control the now skittish animal.

Ben was on the rifle instantly, levering a cartridge into the chamber as Baker, yelling out a warning, tried to get a bead on Ben and control his horse at the same time. His rifle spat smoke and flame and the bullet buzzed past Ben's right ear like an angry wasp.

Ben fired from the hip. The bullet punched a hole in Baker's chest, splintering the ribs before shredding his heart and passing out just below his left shoulder-blade in a crimson fountain. Baker was lifted out of the saddle and slammed to the ground.

Ben tried to lever another cartridge into the chamber, but the rifle jammed and he turned to find himself looking down the barrel of a Walker Colt hefted in Tate's hand.

The man had brought his horse under control and drawn his pistol.

'I owe you one, big boy,' he snarled.

A gun fired and Tate jerked upright in the saddle, a look of surprise on his face as the front of his chest exploded outwards. He clapped a hand to the wound and half turned in the saddle, the Colt slipping from his fingers.

Wes stood there, pistol smoking in his hand.

'Hell an' damnation, it did work,' he breathed in relief, as Tate toppled stiffly from the saddle and crashed heavily to the ground. He made a weak attempt to rise then collapsed and lay still.

Ben threw the useless rifle aside and strode towards his friend, a smile on his big, handsome face.

'Didn't think a few logs would finish you off, Wes,' he greeted happily.

'They sure tried,' Wes returned

lightly. He eyed the horses. 'Looks like we gotta ride into town.'

★ ★ ★

It was dark by the time they reached Mead's Crossing with Sam and Solomon, Wes and Jolene riding double. They left the horses at the livery stable on the edge of town and went the rest of the way to the dock gates on foot. When they reached the gates, they found to their surprise that they were locked.

A crowd of angry people milled before the gates; men clad in elegant frock coats and ruffle-fronted shirts. Gamblers eager for a night at the tables on the *Floating Palace* only to find their hopes and desires dashed. Bidding the others to stay put in the shadows, Wes sauntered forward to join the frustrated mob.

'What's going on here, mister?' Wes addressed a man.

'Duval's taking the *Palace* to New

Orleans for a refit. Business as usual at the Lucky Lady saloon in town 'til she returns.' With that the man pushed past Wes and hurried away.

Those closest to the gates were turning away and Wes caught a glimpse of an armed guard on the other side of the iron-barred gates.

He had heard enough. He hurried back across the street to join the others and quickly relayed the news to them.

'Sounds to me like he's getting ready to run,' Ben said.

'That's how I read it,' Wes agreed. 'The gold must be aboard the *Palace*, hence the armed guards.'

'So whaddaya aim to do 'bout it?' Solomon demanded.

'We need to get aboard the *Palace* and find the gold,' Wes declared. 'How do we do that with the gates closed and guarded, Sam?'

Sam stroked his bearded chin thoughtfully.

'Ain't but one way an' that's by water. There's a slipway leading to the river down by the Steamboat saloon. Allus a couple o' rowboats tied up there, if'n you can row?'

'Pretty handy wi' a canoe,' Ben ventured, earning himself a scornful look from Sam.

'You'll need more'n that, boy.'

'I can row them, Cap'n,' Solomon said.

'We're coming with you,' Jolene spoke up.

'Not this trip,' Wes replied. 'Only a fool puts all his eggs in one basket. In case something goes wrong we need some land-based back-up.'

Jolene's face fell, but she could see the sense in Wes's words and did not argue.

Sam led them to the slipway.

'Shouldn't we be getting help from the sheriff?' Sam asked.

'It's my experience that the local law is a tad reluctant to arrest one of its leading citizens without proof. But if'n we ain't back in thirty minutes — ' Wes gave a bleak smile — 'it might be a good idea to acquaint him with the facts.'

'We'll do that, Wes,' Jolene agreed quickly. 'You boys take care now.'

As Solomon reversed an oar and used it to push them out into the river, Ben called back softly, 'That's what we're best at, ma'am, taking care.'

It took only a few minutes for Solomon to row to the *Palace* and for the two to scramble aboard, leaving Solomon to wait for their return.

'How in tarnation we gonna find the gold?' Ben asked, as they crouched in the shadows of the main deck's cargo area just forward of the big covered side paddle. On the river side of the steamboat the shadows were thickest, but in the dim light that did exist they saw the deck was filled with barrels and the air around thick with the stench of kerosene.

'Guess we look until we find it. It's gotta be a sizeable load, packed in crates.'

'May as well start down here then.'

Moving silently they searched the forward area, but found nothing then they moved to the aft cargo area that turned out to be empty.

'Hell there's more decks above than a big city hotel,' Ben moaned. 'They could be stashed anywhere.'

Wes massaged the back of his neck.

'I'd've staked a week's pay they'd be on this deck. Figure they'd be too heavy to carry to the upper decks.'

'Less'n they used a winch,' Ben replied.

'Mebbe,' Wes said, then he grabbed Ben's arm and in the thin light Ben saw that Wes was smiling. 'Dammit, Ben, we've been looking at 'em and ain't realized it.'

'We have?'

'Sure we have. The *Palace* is a gambling boat, presumably heading to New Orleans for a refit.'

'So?'

'So why is she carrying a cargo of kerosene?' There was a triumphant note in Wes's voice.

'You thinking them barrels are full of gold?' Ben voiced.

'Only one way to find out. Come on!'

They prised off the tops of three barrels before finding one filled with gold bars.

'Mus'' be over fifty barrels here. I wonder how many are filled with gold?' Ben mused.

'Forty-seven barrels actually and thirty-eight contain the gold.' The amused, informative voice had the two spinning around to face the shadowy figure of Cord Duval flanked on either side by the ever watchful Lacroix brothers. 'Please raise your hands, gentlemen, or you will die now.' To accompany his words came the clicking of a dozen or more gun hammers being thumbed back.

Dark figures appeared all around them, some carrying lamps that chased the shadowy darkness away to leave the two exposed. With no other option left they raised their hands.

Duval, still smiling broadly, snapped his fingers.

'Bring them.'

They were taken to the second level salon that inside resembled a western saloon, only far more opulent and luxurious. A long bar ran down one side of the room, its brass footrail polished and gleaming like the gold in the barrels below.

Tables and chairs ran the length of the room that was as long as the old *River Queen* had been. Ornately carved ceiling arches, like the ribs of some fabulous beast, curved overhead, painted gold, and between them hung huge, sparkling chandeliers. There were eight in all, each one lit to fill the salon with a rich, sparkling light.

With the polished wooden floor and alternate claret and silver drapes adorning the walls between the windows, it was luxury that neither man had ever seen before.

Their guns were taken from them

and placed on the bar and Duval allowed them to lower their arms.

He lit a cigar as he sat down at a table, the Lacroix brothers standing either side of him, while behind Wes and Ben stood two more armed guards.

'You boys constantly amaze me. Where's the *River Queen*?'

'What Haggar failed to do, your man Tate succeeded in doing. She's on the bottom of the river now,' Wes answered.

'What happened to Haggar?'

'He tried to ride the Jaws, 'cepting he was a tad too big to swallow whole.'

'What about Tate?'

'Something he ate disagreed with him. Made of lead as I recall.'

Duval chuckled, unperturbed.

'I take it Pepper and his brat are still alive?'

Before Wes could frame an answer there was a noise outside, the door was thrust open and Solomon was propelled into the room.

'Found him waiting in a boat for these two to return,' Solomon's captor cried.

'Excellent, excellent,' Duval applauded. 'Well, well, what shall we do with you three I wonder?'

'I'm sure you'll figure something,' Wes returned.

'I'm sure I will,' Duval agreed. 'Tell me, Mr Hardiman, how did you know the gold was here, in Mead's Crossing?'

Wes told him of his theories, only too glad to keep the conversation going to give Sam time to get to the sheriff.

'Very astute of you and quite correct in every detail,' Duval applauded when he had finished. 'Yes, Blake did force my hand when he stole a gold bar from my safe, but it was time to salvage the remainder of the gold. After twenty years the *Southern Belle* was beginning to break up. If I had waited much longer the gold would have sunk in the mud at the bottom and then been lost forever.

'Time to move on, gentlemen.

England mebbe or France. I look forward to a long and wealthy life, while you three . . . ' He shrugged almost regretfully.

The door burst open for a second time and Sam scuttled into the room, a shotgun in his hands. He was followed by the tall, frock-coated Sheriff Taplow.

'Git your murderin' hands up, Duval. You boys find the gold?'

'We found it, Sam,' Ben called with a smile.

'What did I tell you, Sheriff?' Sam clucked gleefully.

'Drop your guns, boys, or your boss gits his head blowed off. We got a dozen constables ready an' waiting on the dock. Ain't that right, Sheriff? An' Jolene's wi' 'em.'

'That's right enough, Mr Pepper,' the sheriff said, raised his rifle and drove the butt against the back of Sam's head, sending him crashing to the floor.

Duval eyed the prone body.

'You really ought to find out who your friends are, Sam,' he murmured.

It only took a second of distraction. The Lacroix brothers took their eyes off Wes and Ben and the two cowboys reacted instantly.

Wes turned and threw out a foot as his guard bent to retrieve his rifle. His booted heel caught the man in the forehead and sent him tumbling over backwards. At the same time he threw himself on the rifle, grabbing it up, rolling and firing.

Ben was no less slower. He doubled his guard over a fist, caught him by the back of his collar and heaved him towards Duval and the Lacroixs before diving on the rifle.

Bullets splintered the floor as Wes continued to roll, firing and levering as he came on his stomach.

A bullet caught Raphael Lacroix in the face, shattering the front of his skull. The sheriff, retreating to the door, firing wildly from the hip, caught a bullet from Ben's gun in the chest, the impact throwing him hard against the wall.

The dying man's finger reflexed on the trigger and glass exploded from the chandelier above Duval's table. It shattered the oil reservoir container and a flaming stream of kerosene splashed down over the table.

By this time both Duval and Henri Lacroix had dived behind the far end of the bar.

Wes sent a table and chairs flying as he cannoned into them. The table overturned providing a barrier between him and Henri Lacroix.

Bullets ripped into the table top as Ben hauled himself over the bar and dropped down behind it and began firing into the wooden end panel behind which the two were crouched.

Lacroix gave a cry and staggered upright as a bullet tore through his right cheek and out through his left, cutting his tongue in half. Blood erupted from his mouth then a bullet from Wes's gun smashed into his chest sending him sprawling backwards. His heels drummed the floor for a second then became still.

By now dark, acrid smoke was beginning to drift through the salon as the burning kerosene ignited the wood of the table and the floor around it.

'You're finished, Duval. Throw your gun out!' Wes yelled.

A bullet whined close by as an answer.

'Damn you!' Duval cried, rising to his feet, sending a couple of quick shots behind the bar, just missing Ben, before he turned the gun on Wes, but his aim was poor and wild. Wes's aim was more deliberate, but the hammer clicked uselessly on an empty chamber.

Duval laughed and stepped forward. From where he had been huddled before the bar, Solomon rose up. He knocked the gun from Duval's hand, grabbed the man by his fancy lapels and threw him across the room.

Duval hit the burning table that

collapsed beneath his weight. Screaming, Duval staggered to his feet, his clothes on fire.

He tried to run for the door, hit the side and clutched with blistered hands at the drapes to steady himself. The drapes ignited.

Duval went to his knees, his hair sizzling away in a flash. The flesh on his screaming face blistered and burst, blackened as it peeled from the bone beneath. Then he fell forward and lay still.

Wes came to his feet, face white. It was a terrible way to die.

Ben climbed back over the bar and retrieved his and Wes's guns.

'Get Sam to safety, Solomon.'

The Negro nodded and darted to where Sam lay.

Flames were now licking rapidly from drape to drape, curling about the ornate ceiling arches, turning the gold to black as Wes and Ben darted from the burning salon.

The burning of the *Floating Palace*

was an awesome sight that lit up Mead's Crossing until dawn came and took over.

In the cold, dawn light only the main deck remained, piled high with the ashes of the upper decks as they had collapsed downward. Only the tall smokestacks remained, rearing from still glowing ash.

The gold had been saved, the barrels rolled ashore while the upper decks burned. Now the barrels stood surrounded by a ring of constables.

'There'll be a sizeable reward for the recovery of the gold, Sam, an' it'll all be yours,' Wes said.

'But what 'bout you boys?' Sam protested.

'Jus' doing our job, Cap'n', Ben replied.

'Reckon you should be able to buy the best steamboat on the river, Sam,' Wes pointed out.

'What're you boys gonna do now?' Sam asked.

'Head west where life's a tad more

peaceful,' Ben responded, a grin on his soot-smeared face and they all laughed.

THE END

Other titles in the
Linford Western Library

THE CROOKED SHERIFF
John Dyson

Black Pete Bowen quit Texas with a burning hatred of men who try to take the law into their own hands. But he discovers that things aren't much different in the silver mountains of Arizona.

THEY'LL HANG BILLY
FOR SURE:
Larry & Stretch
Marshall Grover

Billy Reese, the West's most notorious desperado, was to stand trial. From all compass points came the curious and the greedy, the riff-raff of the frontier. Suddenly, a crazed killer was on the loose — but the Texas Trouble-Shooters were there, girding their loins for action.

RIDERS OF RIFLE RANGE
Wade Hamilton

Veterinarian Jeff Jones did not like open warfare — but it was there on Scrub Pine grass. When he diagnosed a sick bull on the Endicott ranch as having the contagious blackleg disease, he got involved in the warfare — whether he liked it or not!

BEAR PAW
Nevada Carter

Austin Dailey traded two cows to a pair of Indians for a bay horse, which subsequently disappeared. Tracks led to a secret hideout of fugitive Indians — and cattle thieves. Indians and stockmen co-operated against the rustlers. But it was Pale Woman who acted as interpreter between her people and the rangemen.

THE WEST WITCH
Lance Howard

Detective Quinton Hilcrest journeys west, seeking the Black Hood Bandits' lost fortune. Within hours of arriving in Hags Bend, he is fighting for his life, ensnared with a beautiful outcast the town claims is a witch! Can he save the young woman from the angry mob?

GUNS OF THE PONY EXPRESS
T. M. Dolan

Rich Zennor joined the Pony Express venture at the start, as second-in-command to tough Denning Hartman. But Zennor had the problems of Hartman believing that they had crossed trails in the past, and the fact that he was strongly attached to Hartman's Indian girl, Conchita.

BLACK JO OF THE PECOS
Jeff Blaine
Nobody knew where Black Josephine Callard came from or whither she returned. Deputy U.S. Marshal Frank Haggard would have to exercise all his cunning and ability to stay alive before he could defeat her highly successful gang and solve the mystery.

RIDE FOR YOUR LIFE
Johnny Mack Bride
They rode west, hoping for a new start. Then they met another broken-down casualty of war, and he had a plan that might deliver them from despair. But the only men who would attempt it would be the truly brave — or the desperate. They were both.

THE NIGHTHAWK
Charles Burnham

While John Baxter sat looking at the ruin that arsonists had made of his log house, a stranger rode into the yard. Baxter and Walt Showalter partnered up and re-built the house. But when it was dynamited, they struck back — and all hell broke loose.

MAVERICK PREACHER
M. Duggan

Clay Purnell was hopeful that his posting to Capra would be peaceable enough. However, on his very first day in town he rode into trouble. Although loath to use his .45, Clay found he had little choice — and his likeness to a notorious bank robber didn't help either!

SIXGUN SHOWDOWN
Art Flynn

After years as a lawman elsewhere, Dan Herrick returned to his old Arizona stamping ground to find that nesters were being driven from their homesteads by ruthless ranchers. Before putting away his gun once and for all, Dan forced a bloody and decisive showdown.

RIDE LIKE THE DEVIL!
Sam Gort

Ben Trunch arrived back on the Big T only to find that land-grabbing was in progress. He confronted Luke Fletcher, saloon-keeper and town boss, with what was happening, and was immediately forced to ride for his life. But he got the chance to put it all right in the end.

SLOW WOLF AND DAN FOX:
Larry & Stretch
Marshall Grover

The deck was stacked against an innocent man. Larry Valentine played detective, and his investigation propelled the Texas Trouble-Shooters into a gun-blazing fight to the finish.

BRANAGAN'S LAW
Alan Irwin

To Angus Flint, the valley was his domain and he didn't want any new settlers. But Texas Ranger Jim Branagan had other ideas. Could he put an end to Flint's tyranny for good?

THE DEVIL RODE A PINTO
Bret Rey

When a settler is cut to ribbons in a frenzied attack, Texas Ranger Sam Buck learns that the killer is Rufus Berry, known as The Devil. Sam stiffens his resolve to kill or capture Berry and break up his gang.

THE DEATH MAN
Lee F. Gregson

The hardest of men went in fear of Ford, the bounty hunter, who had earned the name 'The Death Man'. Yet even Ford was not infallible — when he killed the wrong man, he found that he was being sought himself by the feared Frank Ambler.

LEAD LANGUAGE
Gene Tuttle

After Blaze Colton and Ricky Rawlings have delivered a train load of cows from Arizona to San Francisco, they become involved in a load of trouble and find themselves on the run!

A DOLLAR FROM THE STAGE
Bill Morrison

Young saddle-tramp Len Finch stumbled into a web of murder, lawlessness, intrigue and evil ambition. In the end, he put his life on the line for the folks that he cared about.

BRAND 2: HARDCASE
Neil Hunter

When Ben Wyatt and his gang hold up the bank in Adobe, Wyatt is captured. Judge Rice asks Jason Brand, an ex-U.S. Marshal, to take up the silver star. Wyatt is in the cells, his men close by, and Brand is the only man to get Adobe out of real trouble . . .

THE GUNMAN AND THE ACTRESS
Chap O'Keefe

To be paid a heap of money just for protecting a fancy French actress and her troupe of players didn't seem that difficult — but Joshua Dillard hadn't banked on the charms of the actress, and the fact that someone didn't want him even to reach the town . . .

HE RODE WITH QUANTRILL
Terry Murphy
Following the break-up of Quantrill's Raiders, both Jesse James and Mel Becher head their own gang. A decade later, their paths cross again when, unknowingly, they plan to rob the same bank — leading to a violent confrontation between Becher and James.

THE CLOVERLEAF
CATTLE COMPANY
Lauran Paine
Bessie Thomas believed in miracles, and her husband, Jawn Henry, did not. But after finding a murdered settler and his woman, and running down the renegades responsible, Jawn Henry would have time to reflect. He and Bessie had never had children. Miracles evidently did happen.

COOGAN'S QUEST
J. P. Weston

Coogan came down from Wyoming on the trail of a man he had vowed to kill — Red Sheene, known as The Butcher. It was the kidnap of Marian De Quincey that gave Coogan his chance — but he was to need help from an unexpected quarter to avoid losing his own life.

DEATH COMES TO ROCK SPRINGS
Steven Gray

Jarrod Kilkline is in trouble with the army, the law, and a bounty hunter. Fleeing from capture, he rescues Brian Tyler, who has been left for dead by the three Jackson brothers. But when the Jacksons reappear on the scene, will Jarrod side with them or with the law in the final showdown?

GHOST TOWN
J. D. Kincaid

A snowstorm drove a motley collection of individuals to seek shelter in the ghost town of Silver Seam. When violence erupted, Kentuckian gunfighter Jack Stone needed all his deadly skills to secure his and an Indian girl's survival.

INCIDENT AT
LAUGHING WATER CREEK
Harry Jay Thorn

All Kate Decker wants is to run her cattle along Laughing Water Creek. But Leland MacShane and Dave Winters want the whole valley to themselves, and they've hired an army of gunhawks to back their play. Then Frank Corcoran rides right into the middle of it . . .